Lizzie Marlowe
And The Boy From Nowhere

By Chad R Martin

ISBN: 978-1-944583-40-8

Library of Congress Control Number:

This book is dedicated to all the young dreamers out there, and the old ones, who create the magical places, build immersive universes, and keep the thrill of storytelling alive.

Contents

There were many things Lizzie Marlowe refused to believe in—ghosts, horoscopes, and, above all, her Algebra II teacher's ludicrous theory that numbers might possess a sort of "spiritual essence." Yet, as the mysterious boy entered Room 108 that morning, every hair on her arms seemed to dance with a static-like charge, as if teased by the eerie hum of a haunted microwave.

He didn't simply walk, like any newcomer might; he glided across the floor, his movement imbued with a surreal elegance that immediately raised alarms deep inside her. Every stray motion was a silent red flag.

"Class," Ms. Darnell announced, her voice carrying a mix of authority and bemusement as she chewed on her pen cap—a habit that suggested the pen owed her a favor. "We have a new student today. This is… uh…" She peered at a slip of paper, her eyes narrowing in concentration before she flipped it over with a frown. "Asher Quinn?"

The boy offered a slight nod. His chin was smooth and sharply defined, his complexion as pallid and pristine as a sheet of printer paper, while his hair cascaded in the hue of wet ashes. And then there were his eyes—striking silver eyes that gleamed with an otherworldly quality, reminiscent not of mundane gray but of moonlight that had been somehow captured and sealed in a jar.

Asher's attire was immaculate—a button-up shirt pressed to perfection, void of any logos, creases, or any hint of personality. His backpack, too, looked untouched; as if it had been preserved in a state free from the grime of daily existence, unscathed by weather or human touch. The air that trailed behind him carried an oddly compelling aroma—a fusion of sharp ozone and the musty, comforting scent of old library books.

In that moment, every single girl in the classroom blinked in a synchronized rhythm, while half the guys instinctively straightened their seats in silent awe. Lizzie, however, merely squinted at him as though he were a perplexing puzzle missing its most critical pieces.

"You can sit next to Lizzie," Ms. Darnell said, motioning vaguely towards her with a casual yet knowing gesture. "And Lizzie, maybe refrain from interrogating him too much. He's only been in the state for three hours."

A ripple of snickers broke out among a few students. Lizzie rolled her eyes ever so briefly; a flashback reminded her of the time she had once questioned a foreign exchange student about alternate timelines, only to be branded as the local conspiracy theorist. Not again.

With movements so seamless that his shoes produced no discernible sound—impossibly silent against the squeaky linoleum of Southridge High—Asher navigated toward the empty desk beside her. As he sat, his posture was impeccable, regal even; like an ancient statue that had finally learned the secret art of breathing.

Leaning sideways, Lizzie couldn't resist the urge to whisper sardonic humor, "So, where'd you transfer from? Mars?"

Asher turned slowly, his measured gaze meeting hers as his voice, cool and deliberate, slid down her spine like a cascade of icy water. "I don't think I transferred."

She blinked in disbelief. "...You don't think?"

"I simply arrived."

For a long moment, Lizzie stared at him as if trying to decipher a riddle. Asher maintained his calm, his expression as serene as that of a meditating monk. Finally, with a mischievous glint in her eyes, she murmured, "Well, this should be fun."

The strangeness of Asher Quinn deepened throughout the morning. By lunchtime, he had performed three additional acts that utterly unsettled Lizzie:

1. He inscribed words in a language that bore no resemblance to any known alphabet—circular runes interlaced with jagged angles that seemed to shimmer mysteriously when one dared to stare too long.

2. He casually inquired of the lunch lady whether the mashed potatoes contained any "soul matter."

3. And then, as if an unexpected glitch in a film reel, he sneezed and, for a fleeting 0.2 seconds, his entire body flickered. In that split second, he shifted from solidity to transient translucence—revealing hints of bones and all— like a dying light bulb struggling to hold on.

Lizzie had been trailing him in the cafeteria's lunch line when it happened. A soft "achoo" escaped his lips, and just for that brief, surreal moment, his form became an incomprehensible shimmer-pop—one frame he was entirely tangible, and the next, an ephemeral echo of his self. Shocked, she dropped her tray to the floor, but the surrounding chatter remained oblivious.

"Okay," Lizzie mumbled to herself as she fished her phone from her pocket. "New plan: I'm not letting this one slip by." With determined fingers, she snapped a picture of him in the cafeteria. However, when she later reviewed the photo, her heart sank—the image held no trace of Asher. In his place lay merely an empty chair, a still, untouched tray of food, and, bizarrely, a plastic fork levitating about two inches above the table.

Later that afternoon, compelled by a mix of curiosity and trepidation, Lizzie cornered her best friend, Theo. "Tell me you saw the new kid," she demanded, her voice low and urgent.

Theo, nonchalantly biting into a carrot stick, replied, "You mean silver-eyes-no-soul? Yeah, I saw him. He walked right past the AV room, and every monitor there started glitching—even the ancient, clunky CRTs couldn't ignore him."

"So it's not just me experiencing this oddity," Lizzie said, her tone shifting from skepticism to cautious fascination.

"Nope," Theo continued, "I'm thinking he's either a government plant, a ghost, or maybe an alien warlock trying to pass Econ."

Lizzie's eyes narrowed in contemplation. "Or maybe he's all three."

Her gaze drifted back toward the hallway where Room 108 now sat empty, filled with a quiet that was almost palpable. Yet amid that subdued silence, something faint buzzed in the air—a soft resonance, an unmistakable hum that seemed to whisper from deep underground, stirring just beneath her skin.

Lizzie had long dismissed the notion of ghosts and magic, yet she clung fervently to the power of questions. And this enigmatic boy, who introduced himself with the cool simplicity of "Asher Quinn," embodied the greatest question she had ever encountered.

Chapter 2: The House on Quarry Lane

Lizzie wasn't built for lurking in the shadows; she was simply overwhelmed by curiosity. That was the comforting lie she clung to as she slipped behind a dense barrier of overgrown holly shrubs on the corner of Quarry Lane—a street infamous for its cracked sidewalks, an overabundance of chattering squirrels, and that one peculiar house where no one ever stayed for more than a year. According to public records, that house now belonged to a man named Asher Quinn.

Peering cautiously over the top of the hedge, Lizzie's eyes squinted behind a pair of oversized, reflective sunglasses. She hoped they cloaked her curiosity in an aura of casual indifference rather than alarm. The Quinn house stood silently near the end of the cul-de-sac like a perfectly placed punctuation mark—precise, immaculate, and curiously immune to the perils of time. Its white paint was pristine and inviting, the porch railings meticulously straight, the mailbox free of any rust, and no rebellious weed dared disturb the garden.

The home exuded an unsettling sterility, as though its very design had leapt from the pages of a glossy catalog—a house molded meticulously without a breath of real life infused within its walls.

Lizzie stole a glance at her phone, where a blurry map of sinkhole incidents, rendered on a half-glitched geology app, beckoned her attention. Three recent sinkhole collapses had marred a three-block radius of this very street. The latest of these eerie events had occurred just two nights ago and, peculiarly, had been filled in by the county in less than a day—a detail that sent shivers of suspicion down her spine.

Just then, movement captured her attention. The silent hinge of the front door creaked open and out stepped Asher Quinn. Still and composed, he appeared untouched by imperfection. His flawless complexion and deliberate, gliding walk lent him an otherworldly presence. Asher moved toward the edge of the porch, pausing as if carved out of stone, waiting to be awakened. His head tilted just slightly, as though he was listening to secrets whispered by the rustling wind.

Lizzie's heart quickened, and instinct urged her to duck lower. But fate intervened—a brittle branch snapped under her foot, echoing across the silent street. Time slowed as her breath caught in her throat. For a long, tense moment, she remained frozen, every muscle tensed as she peered anxiously through the leaves. When she looked again, Asher had vanished. The once inviting porch now seemed empty, his presence dissolved into eerie nothingness, though the door remained ajar like an unanswered question.

Counting silently—first to ten, then to twenty—the silence deepened to an almost tangible pause, as if the world itself were holding its collective breath. With a defiant shrug to her own courage, Lizzie stepped out of her hiding, crossing the street in light, hushed footsteps. The setting sun cast long, reaching shadows across the pavement, fingers of twilight beckoning her closer. Pausing at the bottom step, her pulse pounding audibly in her ears, she murmured, "Just a peek," as if convincing herself more than anyone.

Ascending the stairs, she pushed open the door and entered a space that felt like a cathedral of mute stillness. The air inside carried a delicate scent—a mixture of copper and the damp promise of rain. The floor lay immaculate, almost unnaturally so, and the walls were painted in hues that defied simple description, shifting subtly as though alive with secret color. There was no clutter, no portrait, no stray mail on the counter—nothing that betrayed daily life. Not even a solitary fridge magnet dared disrupt the orchestrated order.

And then, in the living room, there they were—the Quinns. Positioned with unnerving precision at opposite ends of a long, beige couch, they seemed to be tableaux of perfection. Mr. Quinn donned a pressed navy sweater vest that caught the light just so, and Mrs. Quinn was clad in a floral dress that appeared to be ironed into an almost perfect submission. Both sat unwavering, eyes fixed on a blank, unpowered television screen as if in deep trance.

Neither of them blinked; neither shifted a muscle.

"Uh…" Lizzie's voice faltered at the quiet absurdity, and then, almost as if on cue, they turned to face her.

Their heads moved in an uncoordinated yet simultaneous manner, and in a single, dissonant voice that resonated like a static-laden recording, they intoned, "Asher is not Lizzieilable right now. Would you like to leave a message?"

Lizzie's mind reeled. "What—what are you?" she stammered.

In response, the couple blinked—once, as though a malfunction in their mechanical composure. Their heads tilted ever so slightly, imitating the awkward range of motion of faulty mannequins. In that fleeting, disconcerting moment, Mrs. Quinn's lips opened just a fraction wider than what seemed safe, revealing behind her teeth a glimmer of something metallic and unidentifiably eerie.

Overwhelmed by a surge of terror, Lizzie turned sharply and fled. Her feet pounded the pavement until she was several blocks away, gasping for breath as if she had just outrun a pack of ferocious wolves.

Then her phone buzzed in her pocket. Fumbling it out, she discovered a single text from an unknown number:

stop looking.

There was no signature, just that chilling command. Lizzie stared at the message for long, agonizing minutes before tucking her phone back into her hoodie pocket. Something in this unsettling tableau wasn't right. Not just Asher, nor the unnaturally polished house, and not even those too-perfect parents speaking like a digital recording. There was something far more sinister lurking beneath—a secret patiently waiting, concealed in the stillness.

She needed answers. And deep down, a stark realization had begun to surface: Asher wasn't concealing the truth; he embodied it.

———

As dusk draped the town in smoky violet and the streetlamps awakened one by one, Lizzie found herself riding past the abandoned Crestline Drive-In—a relic whispered about by kids who claimed it was haunted, not by ghosts, but by an aura of bad taste. Though no movie had graced its screen for nearly a decade, the ticket booth lights would sometimes flicker unexpectedly, and several local legends spoke of shadows dancing on the long-dormant screen well after midnight.

Lizzie hadn't planned this detour; her legs had steered her off the familiar path as if guided by an instinct she couldn't quite fathom. Perhaps it was a latent pull from deep within, or maybe something else entirely was summoning her.

She carefully lowered her bike into a bed of tall, whispering grass beside a crumbling fence and hoisted herself over it, the metal groaning under the weight of her step. Dry, brittle weeds clutched at her jeans as she slipped between overturned speaker posts and rusted-out snack carts, moving steadily toward the back of the lot where shadows coalesced like ink pooling on a page.

Then, almost imperceptibly, she detected a subtle hum—a sound so faint it barely registered, as if stirred by an ancient force slumbering beneath the surface. It was a whisper beneath a whisper, a murmur from another time.

And then she saw it.

Hidden behind the shattered remains of the concession stand, obscured by a collapsing plywood wall and a riot of stubborn thorns, the ground revealed an eerie dip—a perfectly slanted ellipse that was neither a natural crater nor a simple hole, but a deliberate tilt in the earth's fabric, reminiscent of a tilted drain inviting the unseen in.

This was no natural formation.

The dirt did not crumble or collapse; instead, it flowed smoothly, almost glass-like, into a darkness that defied expectation. Lizzie stood transfixed, her gaze locked on the impossible slope that bent away from gravity itself, stirring a whirl of apprehension in her stomach. The narrow entrance measured only about three feet across, yet it exuded a profound depth—as if the very spine of the world had fissured open, beckoning her into its secret depths.

The low hum grew more insistent, vibrating not just in her ears but deep within her bones. Taking one hesitant step after another, she edged closer until a sudden shift in the wind and a drop in the temperature made every hair on her skin stand on end.

Just beneath the shifting surface—whether ten feet or a hundred—she caught sight of a pulsing light, faint but rhythmic, echoing the steady beat of a far-off heart.

Time itself seemed to pause as she absorbed this spectral vision. Only when she finally turned to leave did her eyes fall upon something peculiar carved into the crumbling concrete lip of the drive-in screen. Three symbols—one rounded, one angular—were etched there, shimmering ever so slightly as if they recognized her presence. One of the symbols mirrored the pattern Asher had been scribbling in his notebook, a detail too uncanny to ignore.

Swallowing the rising lump of anxiety, Lizzie realized that the mystery was not only bizarre—it was waiting for her, silently pulsing beneath her very feet.

"What in the frickety-frick is going on?!" she murmured aloud, her voice a mix of awe and exasperation.

Without a moment's hesitation, Lizzie swung her leg back over the fence, jumped on her bike, and pedaled with fierce urgency toward home, unaware that in the enveloping darkness, something unseen had been watching her every move.

Chapter 3: The Mirror Moment

"Okay, so listen closely," Lizzie declared, practically gliding into her seat at the far corner of the lunch table as if swept along by an unseen force. "What if the Quinn house isn't really a house at all, but a sophisticated façade? It's just too perfect—like a simulation painstakingly crafted to mimic what a house should look like."

"Good afternoon, Lizzie," Simone Wright drawled, her tone as dry as scorched toast. "Your graceful descent into madness is truly a sight today."

Lizzie dismissed her cutting remark as she fumbled with her phone, its screen lighting up with a blurry photo from the previous day. The image was meant to capture Asher, yet all it revealed was an empty chair, eerily juxtaposed with a lone, floating fork suspended in mid-air.

"I'm telling you, something's off," she insisted, angling the phone toward her friends so they could scrutinize the strange picture. "Just look at this. Look—where is he?"

Simone glanced at the image and shrugged indifferently. "Maybe you just missed him."

Lizzie's finger jabbed decisively at the phone's screen. "I don't miss. He was right there. Right. There," she repeated, her tone laced with urgency.

Across the table, Kai Tran—one of the few juniors known to find joy in the study of ancient history—leaned forward with a skeptical frown etched on his face. "Alright, suppose you're right and this guy is a ghost. Or a demon. Or, I don't know, some kind of vampire barista—what's your plan then? An exorcism during Econ?"

"He's not a vampire," Lizzie muttered, momentarily distracted as her thoughts swirled. "I saw him eating pasta yesterday." She hesitated before adding, "Although he did ask if the mashed potatoes contained soul matter."

Simone's lips curved into a smirk as she quipped, "Maybe that's just the new way of being gluten-free."

But Lizzie's expression remained dark, void of any amusement. "I went to his house," she revealed, her voice a blend of defiance and anxiety.

Kai instantly dropped his soda in shock. "You what?"

"I didn't break in!" Lizzie snapped, then quickly softened, "Okay, technically, I entered because the door was open and it just felt natural, but I couldn't ignore what I saw— his parents are bizarre. They speak in unison, their voices merging in a chilling, mannequin-like harmony. One of them even acted like—like part toaster."

Simone blinked in disbelief, while Kai slowly recoiled, his skepticism deepening.

"I'm serious!" Lizzie hissed, her eyes darting around to ensure no one else was listening. "Something strange is happening in this town. First came the sinkholes, then the erratic flickering of lights, and now this kid who mysteriously disappears from photos—and his mom might as well be part WiFi."

Simone's tone turned teasing as she remarked, "You do realize this sounds a lot like the time you thought Mrs. Dunlap was a lizard woman because of her dry elbows?"

"That wasn't about her elbows," Lizzie retorted quickly. "It was about that unnatural, vertical blinking thing."

Before they could dive further into mockery, the bell rang—a resounding chime that signaled freedom—and the hallway exploded with frenzied chatter. Slipping into the bustling crowd, Lizzie felt both isolated in her conviction and increasingly certain that it wasn't just about Asher anymore. Something far more sinister was rumbling beneath the surface, a hidden current she could almost taste.

Third period was Independent Study, which meant Lizzie was stationed in the library for a forty-minute span, pretending to work on her "Personal Research Project." In truth, she was obsessively sifting through old yearbooks, property records, and geological disturbance reports in search of clues about the Quinn family mystery.

Halfway through her fruitless digital excLizzietion, her fingers suddenly froze on the mouse. There on the screen was another photo—a startling image from Southridge Elementary, Class of 2016. It depicted a second-grader with dark, soft hair, warmly tanned skin, and an exuberant, wide smile. The caption read: Name: Asher Quinn. But this wasn't the enigmatic Asher Quinn who had walked into Room 108 just days ago.

Intrigued, Lizzie zoomed in on the digital image, her eyes widening as she discovered further unsettling details. Behind the cheerful young Asher, faintly reflected in the glass of the classroom's aquarium tank, hovered a blurry silhouette—a boy of similar stature and build, yet marred by an uncanny pallor and an unnerving stillness. His face, scarcely visible, seemed to fix the camera with an unblinking, silent stare.

Lizzie's hands began to tremble. She examined the photo over and over. The real Asher—the one whose presence she had felt—had clearly existed. So who was the shadowy figure that appeared more like him than the lively child in front of her? And why did its reflection seem to harbor a secret of its own?

That night, as darkness draped her room in heavy silence, Lizzie lay in bed with her laptop aglow. The faint light of the screen cast shifting, flickering shadows on her walls. Side by side were the yearbook photo and the cafeteria screenshot—two mysterious apparitions, each a ghost refusing to reveal its full story.

Her thoughts drifted back to the shimmering void behind the drive-in, the strange symbol etched into the screen, and that persistent, eerie hum in her bones. And then there was the chilling message: stop looking.

But she couldn't stop.

With a hesitant click, she returned to the class photo and stared at the reflective glass once more. Slowly, almost as if compelled by a force beyond her control, she reached out and touched the chilled surface of the screen. A sudden, icy shiver raced up her arm and for the briefest moment, the reflection's silver eyes appeared to flicker— as if, in that fleeting instant, it had finally noticed her reaching back.

———

That same night, just a few blocks away, the Crestline Drive-In lay nestled beneath a vast sky smeared with a tapestry of stars, interspersed with low-hanging clouds that drifted lazily by. Behind the concession stand, a slanted opening pulsed rhythmically, as if harboring a hidden heartbeat, with a muted glow flickering from somewhere deep below the earth's crust. The air was thick with anticipation.

And then—

Something stirred beneath the surface. The soil at the lip of the slope shifted and crumbled. A hand emerged—short and thick-fingered, its nails dark, cracked, and sharp like ancient obsidian. It clawed at the earth, pulling its form upward.

The creature that crawled out of the slanted hole was squat and peculiar, no taller than four feet. Its skin was the deep hue of bruised plums, textured like coarse sandpaper, stretched taut over its sinewy limbs. A tangled beard of wiry black hair cascaded from its jaw, interwoven with bits of bone and metal rings, creating a macabre tapestry. Its attire consisted of loose, drab rags, held together with rusted clasps and dusted with a pale green ash that clung to its fabric like spectral powder.

But its eyes—its eyes were alive with fire, burning like smoldering coals. Twin pinpricks of crimson danced with an alertness and urgency beneath a heavy, furrowed brow.

It sniffed the air, the scent of earth and night filling its senses. Then it smiled, a grin that revealed small, uneven teeth—some jagged and sharp, others worn down to nubs by time or use.

The creature turned its head slowly, its neck cracking with a sickening pop, and then it waddled off toward the town on bowed legs. Its bare feet made no sound on the dead grass, its movements deliberate and purposeful. Though hunched, it was far from clumsy, its gait twitchy and reminiscent of an insect's skittering.

As it passed beneath the towering old drive-in screen, it paused, running one gnarled finger over a carved symbol etched into the concrete lip. Its touch was reverent and deliberate.

It whispered something, a low and clicking incantation. The symbol responded, glowing faintly in the dimness.

And then, with the whisper still echoing through the night air, the creature vanished into the trees, heading toward Southridge. Toward the light. Toward the girl who had seen too much.

Behind the gym, the very first sinkhole silently yawned open, as if nature itself had carved a mysterious void in the earth. It didn't shudder, crack, or roar with any hint of fury; instead, it simply appeared—a flawlessly circular cavity nestled in the grass, exactly five feet in diameter and so pitch-black that it looked as though someone had stolen a fragment of the midnight sky and pressed it against the ground.

By the time Principal Hargrove arrived, Coach Jenkins had already cordoned off the ominous site with a circle of vivid, bright-orange cones and strips of makeshift duct tape. The area was strictly off-limits, a precaution born of the fear of an unsuspecting student falling in and breaking something as vital as a leg—or even a piece of school policy.

Lizzie found herself at the taped boundary alongside Simone, both watching as maintenance workers prodded the darkness with slender metal rods, their actions suspiciously reminiscent of gator hunters probing a murky swamp.

In a hushed, urgent tone filled with both fear and conviction, Lizzie whispered, "I'm telling you, this is connected. Everything is interwoven."

Simone, with a languid casualness, popped a tangy Sour Patch Kid into his mouth and replied teasingly, "Connected to what, Lizzie? Your latest obsession—the emotionally unLizzieilable weirdo you insist must be a ghost?"

Lizzie said nothing. Not because she didn't want to answer, but because in that charged moment—when the wind shifted ever so slightly and the distant, throbbing drone of the football team's warm-up faded into silence—she heard it. It began as a whisper; soft, drawn-out, and laden with an ancient, haunting quality. The voice murmured, "Bring him back… complete the self…" and Lizzie's breath hitched as her heart stuttered in response.

"What?" Simone asked, startled by the pause in conversation.

Fixing her gaze on the mysterious void, Lizzie insisted, "Did you not hear that?"

Simone, puzzled, retorted, "Hear what?"

With a casual shake of her head, Lizzie tried to maintain a façade of nonchalance as she explained, "It's nothing… just a little wind," though her voice betrayed her uncertainty. Deep within, she knew it wasn't the wind. The voice had not come from the chilly breeze outside—it had resonated within her, cold and clear, carrying the weight of something impossibly ancient.

Later that day, during fourth period history, Lizzie's eyes kept drifting over to Asher. He sat with an unnerving stillness, his silver eyes locked not on the teacher's lesson but on the pages of his notebook. He wasn't merely doodling; he was deliberately drawing. Intricate symbols unfurled beneath his steady hand—complex, flowing glyphs that interlocked and spiraled in mesmerizing patterns, moving as if under the guidance of an unseen force.

Lizzie craned her neck, striving to decipher every detail, until one symbol in particular—a gracefully curved triangle circumscribed by concentric, looping circles—leapt from the page and caught her in a moment of startling recognition. Her eyes widened as memories stirred; she had seen that same emblem etched into the concrete lip at the old drive-in, the shape and the eerie shimmer tinged with an otherworldly significance. Quickly, she jotted the symbol down on a sticky note before Asher could notice his distraction.

Still, he continued drawing relentlessly, page after page, his fingers trembling ever so slightly while his lips muttered words too soft to be heard. Settling back into her seat, Lizzie felt adrenaline surge through her veins—a silent yet insistent declaration that something ancient was stirring, something that had already touched her soul.

——

Theo Wells took a shortcut behind the school theater on his way to robotics club. A pragmatic skeptic who believed in nothing but hard data, biting sarcasm, and his enviable Fortnite kill/death ratio, Theo found himself confronted by an inexplicable strangeness that day.

It began with the temperature; one moment, a warm, muggy air enveloped him, and the next, the atmosphere plunging as though he'd stepped into a walk-in freezer.

25

Then came a subtle vibration under his sneakers—a soft, rhythmic pulse resembling the measured beating of the earth's own heart. And then, as if summoned by unseen forces, the whisper arrived. It came from right behind him: "Too late... too late to hide..." Theo slowly pivoted, eyes wide with disbelief, only to find the space behind him empty. Yet the air continued to ripple, as though an unseen presence had brushed his cheek, causing his warm breath to condense into misty clouds before him.

Without a backward glance, Theo sprinted the rest of the way to robotics, clenching his secret tightly and vowing never to recount what he had experienced—except to Lizzie.

Later that afternoon, pale and sweating, he cornered her and hissed with urgent fervor, "I think your creepy goblin theories might just be right."

Lizzie blinked in bemused surprise. "What?" she asked softly.

Leaning in closer, Theo confessed, "I heard something behind the theater. It whispered directly into my ear, right into the depths of my soul. I had to run—Lizzie, you know I never run, and I definitely avoid cardio."

Her curiosity piqued, Lizzie pressed, "What exactly did it say?"

After a trembling swallow, Theo replied, "It said it was too late to hide."

Lizzie hesitated a moment, letting the weight of his words sink in before she murmured in a quiet, measured tone, "Then it means whatever is happening—it's just beginning."

They exchanged a glance filled with equal measures of fear and revelation. Lizzie knew she had to uncover the truth before it was too late. She clutched her notebook tightly, determined to follow the tangled thread of mystery until it unraveled completely.

———

Kai Tran was simply trying to head home. Living close enough to school to take the back trail behind the old tennis courts, he normally filled the journey with podcasts or manga on his phone.

Today, however, his phone was inexplicably dead, leaving him alone with a silence that felt unusually heavy as he passed by tangled woods and an abandoned drainage ditch. And then, in that oppressive quiet, he saw it—a hunched figure crouched in the murky confines of the ditch. The figure was small, moving with erratic, twitching motions that sent shivers down his spine.

Kai froze, his heart pounding in his ears, as he watched the creature—no other word could capture its grotesque form—standing about four feet tall with crinkled purple skin, a dark wiry beard, and tattered clothes held together by bone toggles and scraps of chain. Its red eyes glowed faintly as it scanned the drainage pipe, as though searching for something lost. Holding his breath, Kai was immobilized until, as if aware of his presence, the creature slowly turned its head, its glowing eyes locking onto his.

In a flash, Kai bolted at full sprint, his backpack flapping behind him like a parachute, never once daring to look back. He told no one—not yet—but deep down he knew that the creature had seen more than just his face; it had seen him.

———

That evening, as shadows stretched long and sinister across her bedroom walls, Lizzie pored over the symbols she'd seen Asher drawing in class. Her pen traced them again and again on the pages, the lines growing bolder with each repetition until they seemed to vibrate with their own strange life. The curved triangle encircled by loopy rings resonated with an eerie familiarity—it was the same shape from the drive-in screen, she was sure of it. Connecting these fragments felt like slowly turning the gears of an impossibly intricate machine.

She mapped them beside the sinkhole locations she'd found online, her fingers moving with a frantic energy fueled by suspicion and urgency. As she stepped back from the cluttered paper, a cold shiver gripped her spine. The sinkholes formed a perfect triangle around Southridge— the kind that Asher had drawn in his notebook.

The phone buzzed on her desk, startling her out of focused reverie. Its screen glowed ominously with another chilling message from an unknown number: stop...

This time, Lizzie read it carefully before deleting it with defiance burning in her chest, refusing to let fear or threats derail her pursuit of answers. Her thoughts circled back to Asher and his unshakable calm—the way he seemed almost separate from reality itself—and then drifted to that cryptic command that still echoed in her mind: Bring him back... It had to mean something more than it appeared, something she hadn't figured out yet.

Lizzie's resolve solidified like iron under pressure. Tomorrow she would confront him directly; she would lay out everything she'd learned and see if he flinched, if he finally gave anything away.

With adrenaline buzzing through her veins like static electricity, Lizzie stayed up long past midnight, refining her plan over and over in furtive scribbles until exhaustion eventually overtook curiosity.

———

Metallic laughter crackled through the night as a creature skulked its way down Quarry Lane—a path marked by cracked sidewalks and flickering streetlights that cast long, jittery shadows beneath its feet. The squat figure moved purposefully, its beady red eyes scanning for signs of life or interruption.

The Quinn house loomed immaculate at the end of the cul-de-sac, unnaturally pristine against the backdrop of weatherworn homes. The creature sniffed disdainfully at this sterile perfection as it shuffled up the porch steps with feral determination.

It paused at the door but did not knock or ring—simply stood there, smoldering impatience behind its coal-dark eyes. As if sensing its presence, Mr. Quinn opened the door without warning; his movements were smooth yet mechanical, like clockwork obeying unseen commands.

"What do you want?" Mr. Quinn asked coldly, his voice a jarring blend of static precision.

The creature's lips curled into a toothy grin as it hissed in response: "We know you have him... you cannot hide forever."

Mrs. Quinn appeared beside him—her arrival silent but equally dissonant—as they blocked entrance to the house. Their synchronized voices echoed: "He is not yours... We do not fear you."

The creature let out a low, guttural laugh—a sound that rattled through the night like gravel on metal—and then spat back angrily, "You will. You will fear when we come for you."

With a sharp, deliberate turn, it bounded off the porch and into the darkened street. Its limbs moved with an animalistic energy as it wound through the neighborhood, a silent promise lingering in its wake.

The Quinns watched it disappear before retreating into their immaculate abode. The door shut behind them with a harsh click, leaving the cul-de-sac drenched once more in an unsettling silence.

The street outside Kai's house lay in an eerily oppressive silence. Not a single dog barked; not even the slightest whisper of wind stirred the vibrant maple leaves that usually danced in the autumn air. The atmosphere was thick and heavy—as if time itself had slowed, pausing in reverence to the unsettling calm.

Inside, the Tran home ticked like a well-wound time bomb built on relentless routine. The dishwasher cycled with a steady hum, merging with the buzz of a television looping an archaic sitcom laugh track. His parents sat on the couch, unnaturally still, as if frozen by some unseen force. Their rigid silence was too perfect, too deliberate.

Kai stood at the top of the stairs, frowning in mounting apprehension. "Mom?" he called softly. His voice broke the void, yet no immediate response came—only a measured delay. Then, just a moment too late, his mother's head turned toward him.

"Yes, Kai," she said, her voice deceptively smooth and disturbingly rehearsed.

Kai's eyes narrowed in suspicion. "I asked that like five seconds ago."

"We were buffering," his father added with a strangely cheerful note in his tone, all the while keeping his eyes unblinkingly fixed on an unseen point.

A cold shiver ran through Kai as he realized something was gravely wrong—something that had been creeping in all week. The refrigerator inexplicably restocked itself; daily mail that once arrived faithfully had ceased; and, most unnervingly, his parents had stopped sleeping entirely.

His heart pounding, Kai cautiously descended the stairs. "What's going on with you two?" he asked, his voice trembling with urgency.

His mother's smile, widening mechanically, crept across her face as if maneuvered by invisible gears. "We are happy. You are safe," she intoned, each syllable void of genuine warmth.

"You're not even breathing," he whispered, barely audible. At that, the hallway lights began to flicker erratically, casting ominous, stuttering shadows.

In that moment, the corridor behind him transformed. Where moments before there had been a stark emptiness, a tangible darkness began to crawl along the walls—a living void that pulsed and rippled like viscous oil. Within this darkness, dozens of faintly glowing eyes and fleeting, mouthless shapes writhed in an unholy dance.

Then, with a suddenness that mimicked an explosion beneath still water, short purplish creatures erupted from the churning gloom. Their bodies, more solid than flesh and rippling with dark, malevolent energy, burst forth with hellish red eyes. They resembled rabid Smurfs—if Smurfs were transformed into bristling warriors of stone-like muscle and demonic vigor. They were the Hollowkin.

One of the creatures, its limb snapping out like a whip forged from midnight itself, lashed out at Kai. In an instant, the creature yanked him from his feet before he could even muster a scream. His body slammed brutally into the wall, rendering him as immobile as an insect trapped beneath glass. His parents, as though the bond of parental instinct had been severed, remained completely unresponsive—either paralyzed or replaced.

"Help me!" Kai cried, his voice cracking as he thrashed against the overpowering force that held him captive.

In a ghastly display of mechanical precision, his mother slightly turned her head. In that brief moment, Kai saw her face flicker from its human semblance to a ghastly vision of metal and bone beneath stretched, lifeless flesh. Her eyes dimmed momentarily, only to blink back on with a cold, digital regularity.

"You were selected," she stated, as though reciting a predetermined line.

Then, with a collective surge, the Hollowkin advanced. They did not tear or rip with brutal violence; rather, they moved with an unnerving, phasing fluidity—slipping through and around him, erasing his very being as if he were nothing more than an unwanted memory. Kai gasped as numbness crept over his fingers, his thoughts twisting and slipping into oblivion. His eyes rolled back in a final, futile plea for escape.

In the last fleeting moment of clarity, the final, horrifying truth unfolded before him: His parents were no longer his loving guardians. They had been replaced by soulless machina—skin-wrapped puppets designed to mimic love and care in a space where genuine warmth once resided.

And Kai?

Kai was gone, snuffed out of existence as if someone simply turned out a light.

Chapter 5: The Other Side

That night, Lizzie slipped into a dream where falling was an experience of endless descent. It was not that familiar, jarring sense of plummeting panic that sent your limbs flailing and jolted you awake with a racing heart. Instead, this falling was gentle and deliberate—a slow, mesmerizing spiral into darkness, as if countless silver threads crafted from moonlight were tenderly drawing her downward.

She tumbled through vast layers of what seemed like heaven's own veil—clouds that shimmered softly from within, thick and mysterious like a living fog, their interiors dancing with tiny, luminescent constellations that shifted and realigned as she drifted by. There was no scream, no moment of frenetic terror; even if she had wanted to cry out, the dense, heavy air muffled any sound of alarm, as if fear itself had become too weighty to manifest.

When at last her feet made contact with the surface below, she discovered it was not the solid, familiar ground but rather an expanse of radiant light. A plush bed of glowing, velvety moss spread out beneath her, bathing her skin in a soft, pale teal illumination. Every cautious step sent rippling pulses through the earth, as though the ground itself were a living, breathing entity, responding in quiet gratitude. Overhead, the vast dome of this subterranean realm soared upward until it merged with a delicate haze formed by countless dangling crystals and indistinct silhouettes—perhaps birds, or enigmatic creatures masquerading under feathery guises.

The name Acherra echoed in her mind, an inexplicable certainty that resonated deep within her soul. There, at the edge of a sprawling, shimmering forest, she paused. Towering trees stood sentinel in this otherworldly place, their trunks a luminous, pale white that twisted and coiled like intricately braided rope. Their leaves, delicate and translucent, pulsed with an ever-changing palette of colors—lavender, deep blue, and hints of rose-gold— imparting a surreal, rhythmic shimmer as they rustled in a wind that did not exist.

Amid the forest's shadows, small and elusive creatures flitted between the trees. She caught fleeting glimpses of beings with long, silvery tails that flickered like candle flames, eyes that gleamed like polished stones, and scales that refracted light into miniature rainbows, reminiscent of water droplets in a sunlit spray. Some of these enigmatic beings crawled along the forest floor, while others hovered a few inches above, defying gravity. At one point, a creature, roughly the size of a raccoon, locked its gaze with hers; its eyes blinked sideways in a conspiratorial manner before it evaporated into the air with a sound as soft and deliberate as the turning of a page.

Driven by an unspoken call, Lizzie ventured deeper into the realm until the dense forest gradually yielded to a sunlit clearing. In the clearing's heart loomed an ancient ruin—an age-old temple that levitated a few feet above the ground, as if suspended by the forgotten memories of the earth. Ivy and twisting vines wound their way through cracked stone columns, while mysterious, glowing runes adorned the temple steps. These were not static carvings; they undulated and reassembled themselves like a living language, striving piece by piece to speak truths lost to time.

The pull was irresistible. She followed the beckoning call past fields where silver grass bowed respectfully at her feet, across ethereal bridges woven from strands of spider silk and threads of starlight, and through cavernous passages where the very walls pulsed with vibrant veins of shifting color and echoed with unintelligible murmurs.

Along this surreal journey, Lizzie encountered figures— entities that were not entirely human. They appeared as echoes, faint reflections of people whose eyes shone with an unnerving, otherworldly brightness, laden with secrets too profound to share. Some carried soft auras like spectral shadows turned inside out. One such presence was a woman whose face shimmered and rippled like oil on water, her features perpetually evolving, never settling into a single, discernible identity. Despite their intense, almost insistent gazes, these ethereal entities did not hinder her progress.

Eventually, she found herself at the edge of an immense chasm, a yawning abyss whose depths cradled a citadel carved meticulously into the very wall of the world. Far below, intricate stained-glass windows flickered with dancing lights, and colossal statues lined the parapets—

majestic figures adorned with antlers, wings, and countless watchful eyes. One towering statue, its outstretched finger directed downward, seemed to invite her gaze toward a cavern so deep that even the faintest glimmer of light was swallowed whole by utter darkness.

Then, almost as if by magic, a narrow stairway materialized beneath her feet. Without hesitation, she descended this flight of steps, each landing and corner carved into the living rock. The walls were inscribed with ancient, looping glyphs that emitted a faint green luminescence, echoing the soft light of the moss beneath her feet. As she passed, these symbols pulsed with an intensifying rhythm, their glow quickening as if to echo the beat of her own heart, seeping into her skin with an almost tangible energy.

At the bottom of the descending path awaited a stone cell, open yet inescapable in its confining presence. Huddled on the cool, rugged ground of the cell sat a boy whose presence was both familiar and haunting. He was not Asher—but in many subtle ways, he was. His hair was a deeper shade, his skin carried a warmer hue, and his face bore the fractures of unspoken sorrow. Yet, despite these differences, Lizzie recognized in him the unmistakable silhouette of grief and the weight of a silence so profound it cloaked him like a shroud. His eyes met hers, wide and hollow, and in that moment, the unutterable truth of his despair was laid bare.

"I can't get out," he murmured, his voice soft yet resonant enough to seem to shake the very ground beneath them. "Not without him."

Lizzie's heart clenched as she asked, "Who?" even though she sensed the answer buried deep within the shadows of her memory. He offered no explanation. Behind him, etched into the rough stone of the cell's back wall, was the unmistakable mark—a curved triangle circled by looping rings, an ancient symbol pulsing with enigmatic energy.

With a trembling resolve, Lizzie reached out for him. In that moment, their fingers brushed, a connection charged with electric warmth and silent promises. And then, as if reality itself could no longer hold the fragile thread between dream and waking, she snapped awake.

It was still dark in her room. Her sheets were tangled around her as if caught in a storm, her skin damp with the residue of otherworldly cold, and her breath came in ragged, uneven bursts. Yet, as she lay there in the afterglow of her dream, she noticed that her right hand still exuded a faint, comforting glow. For one lingering moment, even in the dark quiet of morning, she could almost feel the warmth of his palm against hers, a memory of connection bridging the realms of dream and reality.

————

Just before sunrise, while the town still slumbered under a blanket of quiet fog, a faint shimmer began to ripple across the grass behind the Southridge High gym. A ghostly aura, almost invisible, wove its way through the mist, resembling a phosphorescent spider web as it hovered over the dew-soaked field.

The sinkhole—still roped off with cones and duct tape—had changed. It had grown larger since the day before and now breathed with a subtle emanation, an eerie reminder of the nightmarish world Lizzie had visited in her sleep. The edges now pulsed softly, rhythmically, like the slow inhale and exhale of some unseen, dreaming beast.

Then, from the darkness below, the first figure emerged. The air around it shimmered, and for a moment, its outline wavered as if struggling through the membrane between worlds. It was short, hunched, and thick-bodied—like a twisted parody of a miner from some forgotten era. Its plum-colored skin was slick with dew, and its beard dragged across the grass like a tangle of wire. Red eyes glowed in the mist as it sniffed the air, then skittered forward on oddly jointed legs, sniffing, searching, grunting.

Two more followed.

One was long-limbed and pale, its arms dangling almost to the ground, eyes wide and glowing with a pale yellow light. The other had no eyes at all—just a slick, slug-like head and rows of twitching fingers that flicked across the earth as it crawled forward. More of them began to appear, their exit a grotesque parody of the school day rituals soon to begin above them.

They were Hollowkin.

Children of Acherra's edges—echoes of fear and curiosity given flesh. They moved silently, sniffing around lockers, scraping claws against rusted vents, brushing invisible trails into the dirt with their crooked limbs. One of them paused at a patch of broken pavement near the bleachers and let out a low, chittering sound—almost like laughter.

Then the sun began to rise.

A pale hint of dawn spread across the sky, casting luminous bands of light that threatened to unmask them. And just like that, they turned. With the same uncanny silence, the Hollowkin slinked back toward the yawning mouth of the sinkhole. One by one they vanished into it, folding back into the dark like pages in a book closing themselves.

The last to leave was the bearded creature—the one who had spoken to the Quinns. It paused at the rim, red eyes flicking toward the sleeping town. It whispered something, too soft to be heard. And then it smiled, baring rows of crooked, darkened teeth. With a twitch, it dropped into the hole, and the earth went still once more.

By the time the sun was fully up and students began trickling in, the sinkhole looked like just another hazard—nothing more than a geological hiccup. But the grass around it was torn. And a symbol—a faint, looping triangle—had been scratched into the dirt by a clawed hand.

Waiting.

Chapter 6: The Hollowkin Warning

Lizzie had rehearsed her carefully prepared speech at least twenty times that morning, each repetition echoing in her mind like a mantra. "Don't freak him out. Don't accuse— simply ask questions gently, calmly. Pretend you're not unraveling on the inside," she reminded herself as she steadied her nerves.

Now, standing before Room 108 with Simone and Theo flanking her like reluctant sentinels, her meticulously constructed strategy began to crumble like sand slipping through her fingers.

Simone leaned close, her tone low and conspiratorial. "He's not just going to confess he's some sort of glowy-eyed nether-doppelgänger. You need to finesse this conversation."

"I am finessing," Lizzie snapped defensively, though her quivering hands betrayed her inner turmoil.

"You're sweating all over," Simone added, her eyes narrowing as she assessed her friend.

"I'm focused," Lizzie insisted, though Theo's leaning against a nearby locker with his arms crossed suggested otherwise. "Focused but unstable. Classic combo," he remarked with a wry smile.

Before anyone could protest, Lizzie moved forward, her determined steps carrying her into the uncertain realm beyond the threshold. Inside, Asher sat at his desk as early as always, a solitary figure enshrouded in quiet concentration as his notebook remained nearly as blank as his guarded thoughts. His pen tapped steadily against the wood, a rhythmic percussion in a language only he seemed to understand.

Lizzie approached with measured, slow steps. Asher did not initially look up from his silent meditation. "Hey," she said softly, her voice unusually low, imbued with a mix of hope and hesitation. Still, he did not immediately meet her gaze. Settling into the seat beside him, she waited until he finally glanced at her, his silver eyes a still, unreadable mirror as he tilted his head in a brief acknowledgment.

"I had a dream," she murmured, her voice tender and laden with secrets. "A dream of an underground world: forests that glowed with an inner light, ruins that floated as if defying gravity, and a boy who looked uncannily like you—trapped in that eerie realm."

Asher's expression remained unmoved, but the familiar tapping of his pen came to a pause, as if even his hand was suddenly uncertain.

Leaning in closer, her voice dropping to an urgent whisper, she continued, "I've seen the symbols you sketch, the ones that haunt the edges of your pages. I know what they mean. I saw one etched behind the old drive-in and noticed the triangle—you keep drawing it over and over.

The sinkholes around town are taking that shape... all around us."

His silence deepened the mystery, though the shallow, measured rhythm of his breath betrayed a hint of trepidation.

In a voice barely louder than a whisper, Lizzie asked, "Are you him?"

At last, Asher met her gaze; his eyes brimmed with a turbulent ocean of unsaid thoughts. When he finally spoke, his voice was soft and trembling, "I don't know who I'm supposed to be."

Before she could probe further, the sound of Ms. Darnell's brisk footsteps filled the room as class began, leaving the weighty questions suspended in the charged air.

——

Later that afternoon, Lizzie found herself alone, the sole student tasked with cleaning out the dusty undercroft of the theater department—a cavernous basement beneath the stage redolent of wet wood, old makeup, and the faint scent of forgotten dreams. The quiet solitude provided Lizzie with ample time to let her mind wander through her tangled thoughts.

While sorting through a jumble of old costumes, shimmering with lost glitter and echoes of middle school performances, the ancient light overhead sputtered and flickered. First it buzzed, then died, plunging the space into a disorienting gloom. Lizzie clicked on her flashlight, its beam casting long, eerie shadows across the hanging clothes racks and peeling set pieces. A sudden sound, like the scraping of claws on concrete—"skritch"—made her heart skip a beat.

"Hello?" she called out tentatively, immediately second-guessing herself as the faint sound repeated, "skritch... skritch... skritch..."

The sound grew louder until a figure emerged from the shadows. Standing nearly six feet tall, the creature was hunched and elongated, its limbs grotesquely spindly, resembling a human outline constructed from bent bones and loose flesh stitched together with coarse wire. Its eyes burned with a dull, unearthly amber glow, and a wide, twitching grin displayed too many teeth, all arranged in a manner both unnatural and terrifying.

It was a Hollowkin.

Lizzie's heart hammered in her chest as she slowly stepped back, the sound of her retreat drowned out by the creature's uncanny, insect-like grace. Its movements were erratic and jittery, like a corrupted marionette under the control of unseen strings.

Panic surged through her, and she turned to run—but the creature was swifter. A clawed hand lashed out abruptly, striking her and sending her sprawling to the cold, hard floor. Her flashlight spun wildly before clattering into darkness.

As the creature loomed ominously over her prone form, a sudden burst of light sliced through the darkness—a searing, radiant pulse that exploded across the room. The Hollowkin shrieked in agony, its body convulsing violently as if electrocuted. With a final, furious lurch, it slammed against a wall, leaving behind a smoldering scorch mark, before dissolving into a wisp of darkness, as though it had been sucked into a void.

Lizzie blinked in stunned silence. There, looming above her, stood Asher, breathing heavily. One of his hands remained raised, emanating a faint, ghostly glow of white-blue light that arced like silent lightning along his arm, restrained seemingly by will alone. His face was ashen, eyes wide with a fear that seemed aimed not at the vanquished creature but at the mysterious power within himself.

"You—" Lizzie began, her voice cracking under the weight of shock.

"I didn't want you to see this," Asher murmured, his tone barely audible against the echoing silence.

"Too late," she whispered, her voice laden with both regret and resolve.

He glanced at his hand as the ethereal light flickered once more before fading entirely. "I don't know how to stop it," he confessed, his admission hanging heavily in the charged air.

In that breathless moment, Lizzie found herself momentarily at a loss for words. Yet, deep within her, an inner resolve stirred, a quiet yet insistent command echoing in the recesses of her heart: Then don't stop. Fight.

Lizzie rose to her feet, her mind a blur of confusion and recognition. She couldn't reconcile the boy she'd met with this—this supernatural figure glowing like a living filament. Yet something in her heart told her she'd known it all along.

"I'm not leaving you to deal with this alone," Lizzie said, her voice gaining strength as she spoke. "Whatever this is, we'll figure it out."

Asher's gaze dropped to the floor, the shadows returning to obscure him. "What if I'm more dangerous than they are?" he asked, his voice tinged with a sadness that seemed to unravel the very air around him.

"Then we'll figure out how to make you less dangerous," Lizzie replied. She reached out tentatively, placing a hand on his arm—the spot where the electricity had danced like liquid light. She half expected it to jolt with static, but all she felt was warmth, tangible and real.

Asher flinched at her touch but didn't pull away. Instead, he met her eyes with a look that was both grateful and deeply afraid. He was about to speak when the muffled slam of the theater doors announced someone else's arrival.

"Lizzie? You still down here?" Theo's voice carried through the basement as he descended the creaky wooden steps.

Before Lizzie could answer, another set of footsteps echoed behind him.

"We come bearing snacks!" Simone called out, holding up a suspiciously familiar box of Sour Patch Kids.

Asher stepped back into the shadows, retreating as though he feared either himself or them—or perhaps both.

Theo emerged around a corner first and stopped short when he saw Lizzie and Asher together. "Holy smokes," he murmured under his breath. "So it's true—you're really hanging out with Silver Surfer?"

Simone came up behind him, taking in the scene with an exaggerated gasp. "Wait—you guys actually found each other down here? Are you making pottery now? Is this Ghost?"

Lizzie rolled her eyes but couldn't suppress the smile tugging at her lips despite everything that had just transpired.

Asher tucked his head, "I have to go." He moved so sudden they were too stunned to say anything.

Theo looked around, "what just happened."

Lizzie felt a guilty pang in her stomach. Asher had saved her life at the expense of his secret. What had it taken for him to do that? For once, Lizzie slumped her shoulders and ushered everyone out, "let's go guys." But as she peered over her shoulder Lizzie thought she could still see the wispy remains of the Hollowkin that Asher blasted still trying to fade into the void.

Chapter 7: Dual Histories

Lizzie wasn't supposed to be in the records room. Yet the idea of being "supposed to" rarely kept her from bending the rules. Over the years, she had learned the hidden secrets of the Southridge Middle-High administrative building: the master key was inconspicuously concealed behind a framed portrait of the school's founder, the HVAC vent in the long corridor emitted a low, steady buzz that masked the subtle clicks of her deft fingers as she picked locks, and if you truly wanted to uncover the truth, you had to stop asking for permission.

Now, crouched in a shadowy, windowless room that reeked of dust and whispered with old secrets, Lizzie squeezed herself between two aging filing cabinets. The musty air mingled with the faint scent of paper and forgotten memories as she rifled through manila folders, their labels scrawled in faded marker reading "Student Incidents 2019–2021." At first, her search felt aimless—until her fingers brushed against a file that made her pulse race.

There, printed in careful, somber lines, was a report that chilled her to the bone:

QUINN, ASHER Age: 10

Date: March 11th, 2020

Status: Missing, presumed deceased

Notes: "Vanished during geological instability. Area closed by city officials. Recovery impossible. Family relocated months later."

The attached photograph hit her like a physical blow. In that moment, she saw him: the real Asher Quinn. His tan skin glowed softly in the daylight, his brown eyes seemed to hold depths of both wonder and sorrow, and his messy hair and shy, lopsided grin spoke of a boy uncertain whether a smile was even allowed. The report noted the incident's location—a nature trail winding behind the old drive-in theater, where a sudden sinkhole had swallowed him whole.

Lizzie's breath caught in her chest. The documentation confirmed what she had long suspected: the real Asher had been consumed by a sinkhole, much like the others that had been mysteriously appearing. The event was marked as coinciding with the onset of the pandemic—a cosmic coincidence, or something far more deliberate? Now, inexplicably, Asher had returned, altered, and the teachers remained blissfully unaware that the boy before them was the same missing child. How could they not connect the dots?

Determined to unravel this mystery, she had to find him. After all, he had just rescued her life from a shadowy creature that prowled in the dark corners of her world. Later that day, she found Asher alone on the bleachers, his presence a solitary figure against the backdrop of an empty football field. He gazed out into the distance, lost in a pensive reverie, as though waiting for memories to resurface from the silence.

He didn't flinch when she approached. "I know who you are," she said in a voice as flat and quiet as the room around them. His silence spoke volumes. Settling next to him, the faint warmth of the manila folder still lingering in her backpack, Lizzie continued, "Asher Quinn disappeared when he was ten. There was a sinkhole behind the drive-in. He never reemerged."

Asher's gaze dropped to his hands, fingers interlaced with a delicacy that belied their stillness.

"You showed up five years later," she pressed softly. "There are no records, no trace of family or past—just an arrival, as if someone had hit the reset button on a lifetime of memories."

His jaw tensed in a silent struggle, yet he kept his eyes fixed on the distant horizon.

"I found the file," she continued, voice trembling with a mixture of curiosity and dread. "It said you were presumed dead, only to be abruptly updated to 'moved away' once you reappeared at school."

Finally, Asher turned his head, his silver eyes meeting hers with a melancholy so profound it nearly stole her breath away. "I am him," he murmured gently, "But I am not him."

Their silence stretched out, long and peculiar, as a heavy wind stirred the scattered leaves on the bleachers below, adding an eerie soundtrack to the moment. "What does that mean?" Lizzie asked in a perplexed whisper. "Then what are you?" Her voice was laced with equal parts exasperation and sadness.

Asher didn't answer with words. Instead, his face softened, transforming from fear to resigned acceptance. It was as if an inward question, perhaps even older than either of them, was finally ready to be faced. "I wasn't supposed to feel anything," he said, his tone laced with an unfamiliar confession. "Not guilt. Not fear. Definitely not... memory. But something's changing. It all began when I saw you."

"Why me?" she pressed, her heart pounding with a blend of hope and aching confusion.

This time, he looked at her—not with sorrow, but with a dawning sense of wonder. "Because you remember him. The real me. Even if you don't know how." Lizzie blinked, taken aback by the revelation. "I never knew—"

He leaned in, his voice lowering to a whisper as if sharing a sacred secret. "But you did," he murmured. "Before the hole, before the void swallowed him. You were there."

A shiver trickled down her spine as fleeting images flared in the recesses of her memory—water droplets cascading through autumn leaves, the sound of a boy's laughter pairing with the beam of a flashlight, a childish drawing etched in the soft, yielding dirt. Before she could voice another thought, Asher rose to his feet.

"If I am the other half of him," he began, "then someone set me free —to pass through life unnoticed, to watch, perhaps even to replace. But if I'm beginning to recall memories that no one ever stamped into me, then that means the unification is happening." He started to walk away, paused, and then turned back toward her with a resolute gaze. "You were right," he stated softly. "This town isn't normal."

And with that, he strode off the bleachers, melting into the gathering twilight, leaving Lizzie not with comforting answers, but with a cascade of questions that churned as unsettlingly as the wind coursing over the empty field. She quickly hustled after him.

"If you're not the real Asher then why did you save me from that creature? And what was that light that came out of your hands?" she asked, hurriedly trying to match his pace.

Asher slowed, glancing back with a conflicted expression. "It was instinct," he admitted, a hint of vulnerability in his voice. "I didn't know I could do that until it happened." His brow furrowed as though contemplating his own existence.

"But you did it anyway," Lizzie insisted, breathless with unwelcome admiration.

"I didn't want you to get hurt," he said simply before continuing on.

Lizzie stopped pursuing, knowing when not to push, but her heart still raced from the exchange. Something had shifted; she felt it deep within—a subtle tilt in her understanding of the world and of herself. She needed to piece this puzzle together before the pieces vanished again.

Simone and Theo were waiting for her at the edge of the field, curiosity burning in their eyes.

"Did Mr. Ghost leave you a spectral love note? Should we call an exorcist?" Simone teased, but her voice held genuine concern beneath the humor.

"Forget love notes," Theo interjected, peering intently at Lizzie. "This is serious, isn't it?"

Lizzie nodded, clutching the folder tightly. "Asher Quinn disappeared in a sinkhole when he was ten. Then he shows up at school five years later, and no one remembers who he is."

Theo's eyes widened with understanding. "You think it's connected to those other holes popping up around town?"

"And those things—the ones that attacked us at school?" Simone added, her skepticism melting away.

"I don't just think it's connected. I know it is." Lizzie's resolve hardened as she spoke. "We're going back to the drive-in tonight."

"For what? A seance?" Simone asked, raising a skeptical eyebrow.

"To follow the leads and see where they take us," Lizzie replied. "Asher's not telling me everything, but I think we're getting close. We need to find out what's really going on before—"

She hesitated, not wanting to vocalize the chilling thought that had surfaced in her mind: Before more creatures come through.

Theo made a face but nodded reluctantly. "Fine—I'll bring flashlights and snacks."

Simone rolled her eyes good-naturedly as she looped an arm through Lizzie's. "Snacks are good—but if one of those weirdos shows up again, I'm using you as bait."

A thought occurred to Theo, "Have either of you guys seen Kai?"

Simone and Lizzie swapped looks, almost guiltily so for not having mentioned his missing from the group earlier.

"Maybe he's sick," Simone said, "we can drop by his house tomorrow after school if he hasn't shown up before then."

Lizzie smiled despite the fear gnawing at her insides. Together they walked into the falling darkness as streetlights flickered to life above them one by one like curious eyes peering into secrets they could only begin to understand.

——

Creatures crept through shadows behind Southridge High once more that night—their movements bolder now than before. They hissed and snickered among themselves without fear of discovery or intrusion from the waking world above.

The sinkhole had been joined by two smaller tears in reality's fabric—one near the bleachers' edge and another between rusted lockers by an old storage shed across from the gymnasium. Each vibrated with an aura teetering on visibility—an energy so slight it almost seemed imagined until it settled itself into shape—just enough disturbance left behind for anyone attentive or suspicious enough to notice what lay beneath.

Hollowkin emerged from each fissure; some short and stubby, others tall and spindly, some with hairless, gleaming scalps like polished stones. They moved with a manic energy—searching, sniffing, poking into the corners of a world they were only beginning to unsettle.

And for a while, they were alone in their eerie revelry.

But when the night grew deeper and colder, just before they would have retreated back into their hidden domain with newfound knowledge of this world's weaknesses, a light filled the sky above them—a soft but brilliant glow that pulsed like lightning contained in a glass jar.

The Hollowkin paused.

The glow resolved itself into a shape—a figure standing on the roof of the gymnasium. The boy. The uncanny replica. The twin they had failed to claim long ago.

Asher Quinn stood silhouetted against the night sky—his hands raised and radiating an aura that crackled with static intensity. He was more than an echo now; he was dangerous. And for the first time since their arrival, the Hollowkin felt uncertainty take root where confidence once flourished.

Then he unleashed it.

A blast of blue-white light erupted from his outstretched arms, arcing toward them like a meteor shower drawn by magnets' invisible force. It struck the ground mere feet from where they huddled together—a searing wave that surged outward in concentric circles, driving them back with its unearthly power.

The Hollowkin shrieked as one entity—an agonized chorus saturated with fury and fear—and then scattered like leaves torn from branches by wild winds. They scuttled back to their holes and leapt into darkness while Asher's light followed them like molten rivers carving paths through stone.

When silence returned at last, when only charred grass remained where they had stood moments before, Asher lowered his arms and let his breath come ragged between clenched teeth. He did not know how he had done it; he only knew that he must learn to harness this new strength if he hoped to protect those who were beginning to matter again—the ones who dared remember.

He turned away from scorched earth below him—the place where shadows were born anew—and climbed down from the roof as quietly as he had appeared.

Chapter 8: Echoes Below

The morning began in a most peculiar fashion. It wasn't the typical "Asher glitched through his reflection" kind of odd—it was a kind of absurd, offbeat strangeness, as if the universe had rolled its cosmic eyes and chosen the least dignified stage imaginable: Galaxy Strike Lanes on a rambunctious field trip day.

Southridge Junior High's science class, with its mismatched blend of curiosity and chaos, had been unexpectedly rewarded with a trip to the local bowling alley. The official reason was "academic achievement and positive behavior," though Lizzie suspected the teachers really meant, "Let's corral them into an arcade before Mr. Wally's lab experiments go awry once more."

Inside, the atmosphere was dim and flickering under the glow of aging neon lights. The floors carried the unmistakable scent of powdered cheese dust mingled with the warm, lingering aroma of melted wax. In one corner, a dented vending machine lay broken, its contents strewn across the floor like a scattered promise.

Theo pulled Lizzie to the side, "I called Kai's house. It was weird."

"What do you mean?"

"You know how his parents are, super friendly, LOVE to talk, like you can't get them off the phone to talk to him because of how much they like to talk…"

"Theo, I get it, they're talkers," Lizzie interrupted him.

"But that's the thing. Mrs Tran was short, almost robotic. 'He's sick. Won't be in class today.' It was weird."

That caught Lizzie off guard. It was eerily similar to Asher's parents. She wouldn't get a chance to press Theo further as their teacher began speaking to the group.

"Alright, class," Mr. Wally announced in a nervous murmur, his voice jittery like a tiny, half-bald figure with unruly curly hair, "choose your lanes. You've got two hours, and I'll be waiting in the lounge."

Lizzie, Simone, Theo, and Asher settled beneath a flickering neon sign proudly declaring LANE 7: Galactic Thunder. Simone, with dramatic flair, was in the midst of an elaborate pre-roll dance routine, complete with flashy finger-guns, a confident shimmy, and lip-syncing the electrifying lyrics of "Toxic" by Britney Spears. With a flourish that suggested she was performing on a grand stage, she launched her bowling ball down the lane—only for it to clang dully into the gutter halfway along its course.

"Galactic disappointment," Theo muttered dryly as he sipped his bright orange soda, the bubbles dancing in his cup.

Simone spun around dramatically. "I'm just warming up," she declared, her voice tinged with a mix of brLizziedo and playful defiance.

Theo's frown deepened. "You've been warming up for an hour, Simone."

Lizzie chuckled softly at their banter—but her laughter died as an eerie, static buzz crawled up her spine. Something felt off. She turned just as the light above the soda machine sputtered and died, replaced for a split second by a deep blue flare before snapping out entirely. At the front of the alley, the neon "OPEN" sign stuttered, glitched, and then erupted in erratic sparking. The lights began flickering in and out of existence, causing a bout of joyous hysteria among the other students.

"Asher?" she whispered, her tone suddenly cautious.

He was already transfixed, his gaze fixed on the far wall of the alley, his eyes narrowed in alarm. And then it happened.

Out of the darkness, a Hollowkin emerged, bathed in the sickly glow of a black light. It crept from between the arcade cabinets, where the shadows pooled deepest. It was not as tall as the monstrous being that had once attacked her beneath a stage—it was squat and jittery, its movements mechanical, as if animated frame by excruciating frame. Its skin bore the mottled purple hue of an old bruise, and its mouth twisted into a cruel, rictus grin. The creature's glowing red eyes locked onto Simone, who stood frozen mid-dance, one hand still posing in a practiced, jazz-like gesture.

"Is that... a kid in a costume?" Simone asked slowly, her voice laced with disbelief.

"Nope," Theo breathed heavily. "That's definitely not a kid."

The creature edged forward with an ominous hiss that seemed to vibrate in the stale air. Without warning, Lizzie shoved Simone back and lunged for the backpack she had nearly left on the bus—a bag that now felt almost like a lifeline.

"Asher," she snapped urgently. "Now."

Without a moment's hesitation, Asher's eyes flashed with a surreal silver-blue light as his hand pulsed with an inner radiance. He thrust his hand forward, unleashing a jagged burst of energy that arced across the floor like a bolt of celestial lightning. The Hollowkin shrieked, its body convulsing as it skittered sideways with unnatural speed. It darted behind a rack of discarded rental shoes, sending them crashing in a disarray of plastic and fabric.

Instantly, pandemonium ensued. Screams of panic rose as children scattered in every direction. Bowling pins clattered to the floor in a chaotic cascade, and an employee dove behind the counter, shouting about "prank apps" and "calling corporate" in a state of disoriented hysteria.

The Hollowkin, not yet content to retreat, lunged once more. This time, Lizzie was prepared. From her bag she retrieved a curved shard of glass taken from the drive-in— a piece etched meticulously with a looping triangle glyph. As she held it, the shard pulsed softly in her palm, warm and humming with an almost sentient energy.

As the creature neared, it suddenly jerked as though struck by an invisible wall of force. It recoiled, its shriek piercing the charged air, and began to shimmer violently, as if its very outline was breaking apart like heat waves rising off hot asphalt. Asher raised his hand again, and this time the light pulsing from his fingertips intensified, flooding the entire lane with a harsh, colorless brilliance. In the blink of an eye, the Hollowkin disintegrated mid-lunge—as if it were nothing more than smoke being sucked into a powerful vacuum.

In the ensuing quiet, the silence was almost deafening. Then, as if nothing had happened at all, the jukebox sputtered back to life, blasting out the cheerful strains of "Dancing Queen."

Simone blinked in amazement. "Did I just almost get murdered in bowling shoes?"

Theo, collapsing into a wobbly plastic chair, gasped, "Okay. That was too much cardio for one day."

———

Later that night, refusing to wait for an invitation, Lizzie found herself standing at Asher's house. The wind whipped sharply around her as she stepped onto the porch of the impeccably perfect home on Quarry Lane—a structure so precise it seemed as though every line had been drawn with a ruler before being scrubbed clean of any trace of history.

She knocked once. No one answered. She knocked a second time, and this time, the door swung open silently.

In the dusky hallway stood Mr. and Mrs. Quinn, their hands neatly clasped as if they had been awaiting her arrival all along.

"We weren't expecting any visitors," Mrs. Quinn said in a voice that was calm, measured, and disconcertingly metallic.

"I need to talk to Asher," Lizzie insisted, stepping inside without waiting for permission.

"We do not advise—" Mr. Quinn began, his tone hinting at caution.

"I wasn't asking," Lizzie cut him off sharply.

The Quinn couple paused, their movements stuttering like buffering files, and Lizzie slipped past them into the dimly lit living room where she called out, "Asher."

He was already there, standing barefoot at the top of the stairs, his gaze fixed on her with eyes that shone silver and strange—a softness mingled with an unexpected sorrow.

"You came," he said quietly.

"You saved me. Again," she replied earnestly. "And I still don't know what you truly are, but I think I'm ready to find out."

Mrs. Quinn looked at them both with lifeless eyes that seemed to focus on everything and nothing. "This young lady is rude."

"And impulsive," Mr. Quinn added in the same tone.

"We like her," the finished together.

"Um, thank you, I guess..." Lizzie said confusedly.

A long silence stretched between them until Asher began his descent down the polished wooden stairs, his bare feet making barely a whisper as he moved. As he passed by his "parents," they turned slowly to face the wall, freezing in place like mannequins that had been unexpectedly powered down.

A chill ran down Lizzie's spine as Asher extended his hand towards her. "Come with me. I'll show you."

"To where?" she asked, her voice barely above a whisper.

"To the place I come from."

They did not exit through the front door. Instead, Asher led her quietly through a back entrance, guiding her past pristine hedges, across a flawless expanse of lawn, and down a gravel path that Lizzie had never noticed before. The trail twisted mysteriously behind the property, past an old, weathered shed, and into a dense copse of trees.

After what felt like an eternity of wandering, they arrived at a hill that sloped unnaturally and nestled into its base was a narrow slit in the ground—an opening so subtle it might have been missed by the unobservant eye. The faint shimmer of moonlight outlined the gap, hinting at secrets hidden beneath the earth.

No longer merely a slanted hole, it revealed itself to be the one true passage. Asher knelt beside it, pressing his hand to the cool, damp dirt, and whispered words in a language that Lizzie did not understand but that resonated deep within her bones. In response, the ground pulsed gently, and the narrow opening widened as if awakened from a long sleep.

Beyond lay another world—a realm painted in pale hues of green, lavender, and blue, where the light pulsed rhythmically like the vibrant veins of some ancient, living creature. Asher turned back to her, his eyes gleaming with determination.

"This is the way in," he said softly.

Lizzie inhaled deeply, her heart pounding with anticipation and quiet fear. And with that, she stepped forward, into the embracing darkness of the earth, towards a destiny that lay far beyond the familiar confines of her world.

Lizzie anticipated nothing but darkness. She had expected to crawl on her hands and knees through a stifling gloom— perhaps to feel the rough brush of damp roots or cold, unyielding stone against her skin. Yet what greeted her was not the expected tactile obscurity but an overwhelming silence. Not the absence of sound, but the presence of a soft, persistent hum that seemed to vibrate just beneath her skin like Earth's quiet pulse.

The tunnel stretched before her, gently sloping downward without a trace of dirt or scattered rocks. Instead, its floor resembled a smooth, glassy surface that shimmered faintly beneath her boots, akin to ice patterns on a moonlit pond. The walls curved gracefully around her, their semi-transparent surfaces pulsing with glowing veins of violet, aquamarine, and pale green, resembling bioluminescent roots entwined within living crystal.

Beside her, Asher proceeded in a silent yet unwavering pace; the subtle glow bathing him in silver highlights that danced across his features. When Lizzie whispered, "How far down are we?" his response was a mere silent gesture, a pointed look toward the unknown depths ahead.

Soon, the tunnel constricted into a threshold—a slim, rippling veil of silvery liquid that hung suspended in midair like a delicate sheet of moonlight. As Lizzie stepped closer, the fluid barrier shimmered invitingly, and within its undulating surface she thought she detected a reflection—a vision of herself. Yet it was not a perfect mirror image: the girl in the reflection was unmistakably her, yet there was a disconcerting quality about her, as if she were simultaneously older or perhaps even younger. Her eyes faintly glowed, and her skin was traced with looping glyphs, etched delicately like frost along her shoulders. With a hesitant blink, the mysterious image dissolved into nothingness.

"You have to breathe in," Asher said softly, his voice a hushed command that sliced through the charged atmosphere, "not out."

Lizzie, puzzled, managed only a quiet, "What?"

"Trust me," he urged, his tone imbued with quiet confidence.

After a long moment of hesitation, she exhaled slowly and then drew a deep, deliberate breath. The instant her lungs filled with that precious air, the liquid barrier rippled as if in greeting—and then it accepted her. The sensation was not akin to plunging into water but rather like being gently absorbed; her vision blurred into a cascade of smeared colors, and the ambient hum of sound evaporated into silence. In what felt like an interminable moment, her foot connected once more with solid ground.

Lizzie gasped, staggering forward as she emerged into a realm entirely different from the claustrophobic tunnel she had just left—a world alive with radiant energy. They now stood in a colossal cavern whose vast, domed ceiling disappeared into a hazy sea of soft luminescence. The cavern walls were adorned with clusters of crystalline formations that pulsed with a warm, rhythmic light, each glow echoing the distant beat of a subterranean heart. A tender breeze drifted through the space like a whispered secret, teasing the luminous grasses that carpeted the cavern floor in sumptuous shades of violet and mint.

To their left, an immense forest towered—majestic white trees with twisting trunks and leaves crafted like delicate glass, their branches clinking together in a soft, musical harmony. Amid these arboreal wonders, glowing insects meandered lazily, trailing delicate motes of splintered gold light in their wake. To their right, the landscape gracefully descended into a sprawling basin, dotted with shallow lakes that shimmered with otherworldly radiance—some bathed in green, others tinged with lavender, and still others mirroring the sky with haunting precision. At the water's edge, small, foxlike creatures with feathered accents and flickering eyes drank delicately, their reflections dancing and undulating with every subtle movement.

Above all of this surreal splendor, hovering in midair like relics of a forgotten age, were ancient, floating ruins. These weathered stone structures, carved with enigmatic glyphs, rotated slowly as if orbiting an invisible axis, evoking memories of ancient temples or lost civilizations.

"This…" Lizzie whispered, her voice trembling with a mix of awe and disbelief. "This can't be real."

"It's as real as we are," Asher replied quietly, his words carrying both reassurance and mystery.

As Lizzie turned to study him, she noticed that his own radiant glow had intensified amid the cavern's ambient luminescence. His skin caught and refracted the light, his eyes shone with an inner brilliance—as if this magical realm recognized him as one of its own.

Continuing their journey into the heart of the basin, a colossal sculpture eventually came into view—a massive, cracked stone hand surging upward from the ground with its fingers curled yearningly toward the sky. Encircling its base were soft, glowing rings etched with mysterious symbols, orbiting like celestial moons caught in an eternal cosmic dance.

"What is this place?" she breathed, her voice barely carrying over the gentle rustle of the luminous grasses.

Asher paused, his eyes locked on the enigmatic relic, before he leaned close, whispering, "Home."

And in the distance, among the softly glowing trees, something enormous stirred—a silent presence, watching with immeasurable patience and waiting in the enveloping glow of this mesmerizing new world.

Chapter 9: The Doppel Rule

Lizzie had never experienced quiet so profoundly loud. Each step she took across Acherra's moss-soft, velvet-like ground set off tiny, rhythmic pulses through strands of glowing grass. Every gentle breeze that rustled the crystalline trees released a cascade of sound, reminiscent of delicate wind chimes fashioned from whispers. Yet the sensory overload was not solely due to the captivating beauty—it was the heavy, unspoken realization that she had left behind the familiar and crossed into a realm that pulsed with something far older, something ancient.

Beside her, Asher moved slowly, his eyes casting vigilant glances over an ever-changing landscape, as though he were discovering it anew even as he recalled it by heart a thousand times over.

"Where are we going?" Lizzie inquired softly, her voice hushed and full of wonder despite the lack of any overt danger.

"There's someone we need to talk to," Asher answered in a measured tone that resonated with both urgency and reverence.

"Who?" Lizzie persisted, her curiosity tinged with awe.

"She… keeps the history," he replied, his words heavy with the weight of secrets long held.

Their path wound through a grove of trees with glass-like bark that shimmered in the light. When their fingers brushed the exposed, humming roots, a low, resonant melody seemed to rise from the earth itself. Ethereal creatures—some darting with scurrying urgency, others gliding gracefully on unseen currents—flitted in and out of sight, their eyes too knowing to be attributed to ordinary beasts.

Before long, they arrived at a structure carved meticulously into the side of a gentle hill. The dwelling, dome-shaped and enigmatic, was entwined with languid vines that glowed a faint blue, coiling around it like living veins. Over its doorway, ancient glyphs floated and rearranged themselves in a silent dance as Asher approached, as if acknowledging his presence in this timeless sanctuary.

The door exhaled a soft, almost imperceptible sigh as it creaked open, inviting them into the mysterious interior.

Inside, the air enveloped them in comforting warmth, redolent of dried herbs and the crisp, clean scent of ozone. Scrolls drifted through the space, slowly rotating as if suspended in their own small vortex of time, while bioluminescent feathers hung like serene, slumbering birds from the high, vaulted ceiling.

At the heart of this dreamlike chamber, a woman sat serenely—her hair long and white as delicate parchment, her skin illuminated with an ageless, gentle glow. One of her eyes shone with a deep violet hue, while the other refracted light like a living prism. With a smile that held both welcome and quiet command, she greeted them, "You brought her."

Asher paused at the doorway, while Lizzie stepped forward with cautious determination. "Who are you?" she asked, her voice trembling with a mix of anticipation and uncertainty.

"I am called Meridra," she replied, rising slowly with an unmistakable dignity. "Keeper of Names. Recorder of Merges. I retain the memories that others dismiss or forget."

Lizzie's brow furrowed. "Merges?"

Tilting her head as if savoring a fine mystery, Meridra answered, "You have already begun to understand, haven't you?"

Lizzie's eyes shifted to Asher, who remained rooted in a silent, tense watchfulness.

With a graceful sweep of her hand, Meridra directed their attention toward the wall. A subtle ripple shimmered through the air, and soon an illusion took shape—two figures, identical in every detail, standing face-to-face in quiet, profound communion.

"One from Above," Meridra intoned softly, "and one from Below. Each born of thought, memory, and soul—divided by the fragile veil of waking and dreaming, of surface and root."

As the phantom figures drew closer, they merged in a burst of radiant golden light, a union that spoke of a deep communion uniting disparate parts.

"They are reflections, not enemies," Meridra observed. "When they join willingly, they form one true self—a melding of memories, talents, and understanding. Even magic is shared in that unity."

"But if they don't merge?" Lizzie's voice trembled as she posed the question.

Meridra's gentle smile faltered into solemnity. "Usually, nothing occurs because merges are exceedingly rare. The opposites exist in their separate worlds—aware of each other only in the slimmest threads of dreams. Yet when a merge begins, it must be seen through. If it remains incomplete—if one resists the union or if fear fractures the bond—madness can erupt. Or, worse still... oblivion."

The projected illusion shifted. Now, the two forms reached out to touch and began to combine, but then the process stuttered and flickered. One form emitted a soundless scream, while the other began to disintegrate into a scattering of light and shadows.

Lizzie shivered at the vision, the gravity of failure and loss resonating deep within her.

"And Asher?" she asked softly. "He's...?"

Asher stepped forward into the luminous space, his voice barely above a whisper. "I am that opposite here," he confessed, "the echo of the Asher who vanished from your world—a victim of fate, much like the Asher you once knew, ensnared by the chaotic randomness of a merge."

"But you are more than an echo," Lizzie countered, her tone soft yet urgent. "You think, you feel... you're alive."

His voice caught in the delicate balance of vulnerability and fear. "I am scared. If I ever encounter the real Asher— if our paths overlap—what if I lose everything I've become? And worse, what if we fail to find each other completely? Would it lead to insanity, or even death?"

Meridra approached him tenderly, placing a warm hand over his heart as if to steady his beating soul. "You were never destined to become anything fixed," she murmured, "yet you have, and that, dear Asher, makes you far more than an echo."

Asher closed his eyes, seeking solace in the quiet confines of his inner world.

Lizzie stepped nearer, gently brushing her hand against his as if offering reassurance. "You are so much more," she whispered, struggling to capture the perfect word—alive, vibrant, real.

Meridra's soft smile deepened with understanding. "That is because he is home now, in his true realm. Your world has weighed on him heavily, like a dense steel plate pressing slowly upon his very essence."

Asher's eyes opened, now alight with a piercing, silver brilliance. "Then why do I still feel as if I am on the verge of breaking?"

Lizzie's brow furrowed with both confusion and concern as she posed another question. "How did he ever arrive in our world? And what about those bizarre parents—so clearly not human, by the way?"

For the first time, Meridra's gaze softened with a fatigue born of ancient sorrow as she turned away. "I sent Asher to your world to protect him," she explained quietly. "Those machina you mention are nothing more than replicates—facades meant to conceal the truth. I had hoped that our Asher might find yours and merge, saving both from a destiny of insanity or death."

"But the Asher from my world disappeared five years ago," Lizzie recalled, her voice heavy with regret. "They said he fell into a sinkhole that opened suddenly without warning."

Meridra turned slowly, her eyes reflecting a deep, inscrutable sadness. "You say the boy went missing in a sinkhole? I do not understand…" she murmured, her head shaking slowly in disbelief.

With careful deliberation, Lizzie retrieved a worn article from her backpack and handed it to Meridra. The keeper of history read the familiar lines repeatedly, her eyes scanning each word with deliberate sorrow before returning it to Lizzie. A bleak expression rippled across her ageless face. "What is it?" Lizzie asked softly, the question heavy with unspoken pain.

Drawing a long, steady breath, Meridra spoke in a hushed, respectful tone, "I remember that incident well. But the only recoveries we ever made were of the parents—there was no boy among them."

"Recovered?" Lizzie echoed, a chill of finality in her tone.

"Yes, dear," Meridra replied in a quiet whisper reserved for truths too heavy to utter aloud. "They were found, and they were deceased."

In that moment, the ancient words lingered in the air—a solemn echo of loss and transformation amid the shimmering tapestry of a world where beauty and peril danced side by side.

"Then he…" Lizzie's voice faltered, the weight of Meridra's revelation crashing down like an Lizzielanche of truths. "He never made it out?"

The room seemed to tighten around her, the soft hum of Acherra's vibrant energy now deafening in its insistence.

Meridra's gaze softened with a deep, enduring sadness. "It appears so," she whispered, her voice barely audible over the rhythmic pulse of the suspended scrolls. "I fear he is still trapped below—the initial surge of a merge that went wrong."

Lizzie felt as though the ground had been pulled from beneath her feet. "He was supposed to be gone forever," she said numbly. "Everyone back home thought he'd died."

"And he will be," Meridra replied with a solemnity that seemed to echo through the ages. "If the merge is not completed soon, your Asher will dissipate entirely."

"That was five years ago!" Lizzie exclaimed, "he never came back to our world."

Asher turned away, his hands clenched into fists at his sides. "So there's no hope for either of us if we don't find him," he said bitterly.

Meridra placed a gentle hand on his shoulder. "You still exist," she said softly, "which means he does too. You must find him—allow your consciousness to bleed through his before it's too late."

Lizzie struggled to swallow her rising panic, images of her childhood slipping through her thoughts like forgotten dreams now painfully reborn: moments spent playing in sunlit parks with a boy whose presence she had somehow always known was missing from her life—a boy who had left an indelible mark even in absence.

"What about those... things?" Lizzie asked, forcing herself back into focus. "The ones hunting us? The creatures that came through?"

"They are Hollowkin," Meridra explained, casting a wary glance toward the door as if expecting them to burst inside at any moment. "Reflections without soul—unanchored echoes desperate for substance."

"They're trying to take him back?" Lizzie asked, nodding toward Asher.

"Yes."

"But why?"

Meridra considered the question carefully. "They are more than just monsters—they are the manifestations of echoes and greed, envious and driven by desire for permanence—

for stability and existence in our world. They live in the fringes. And every once in a long while, a doorway anchors both or our worlds and they are able to get through. They feed on your fear, on your anger, on all the negative emotions. They rot the soul then feast upon it."

"They've been underground? In hiding?"

"Not always underground," Meridra corrected softly. "There was a time when they roamed free above as well—until they were banished here long ago by an ancient order who feared their instability more than you could imagine."

"Avelynn," Lizzie breathed aloud suddenly—the name reverberating from some distant memory.

"Yes," Meridra replied gently. "Avelynn—a city on your side built by those who knew our world better than anyone else."

"And now?" Asher asked.

"Now they have found a way back through unintended errors in reality—and they want you because you are their chance at true form and surface freedom once again."

"So what do we do?" Lizzie demanded urgently.

Meridra gave them both a long look filled with equal parts sympathy and resolve: two halves that did not yet realize how deeply intertwined their fates had become.

"You must find him," she repeated with quiet insistence. "Before they do."

Asher looked at his hands, "but what about these powers?"

"Powers?" Meridra asked in surprise, "yours are manifesting?"

"Yes," Asher looked at her desperately.

"Then the hour is later than I feared. Wherever Lizzie's Asher is we must find him. I will visit the diviners, perhaps they can help. There has to be something we missed the day the sinkhole swallowed his parents. Until then, you must both be safe and be vigilant, if the Hollowkin are crossing over as you say, then something bigger is at hand."

——

The night was cold but bright as Lizzie and Asher emerged from Acherra's depths—the moon casting long shadows on the cracked sidewalks of Quarry Lane.

Simone and Theo waited for them on the corner, pacing anxiously under a flickering streetlight.

"Where have you been?" Simone demanded as soon as she saw them. "We've been calling all night! Your phone goes straight to voicemail!"

Theo crossed his arms. "We thought you'd disappeared into some cosmic black hole."

"Not yet," Lizzie said breathlessly. She launched into an explanation of the world below—how two halves tried to make themselves whole, how Asher was one part of a divide forced apart by tragedy.

Theo's eyes widened as he listened. "So there's another Asher? And he's alive?"

"We think so," Lizzie replied quickly. "But we need to find him before those creatures do."

Simone looked skeptical but intrigued. "And if you do find him? How exactly are you going to deal with... all this?" She waved her arms vaguely in the air—encompassing not just the mystery itself but its impossible scope.

Asher took a deep breath.

"We don't know yet," he admitted quietly. His voice held both hope and doubt. "But we have to try."

They set off together through the sleeping town—their footsteps echoing against empty streets that seemed almost too still beneath the brilliant sky.

And then: a sound that shattered silence like glass.

It started low—a rumble barely audible except in its trembling—from somewhere deep below—and then rose rapidly into a deafening roar as earth shook beneath their feet.

"Sinkholes!" Theo shouted as they stumbled backward from a widening chasm directly ahead—one that opened with surgical precision right in front of them before slamming shut again just as quickly—leaving no trace behind except for scattered gravel and dust-filled air.

Lizzie caught her breath first—and something else: movement across the lot where it had happened—a figure darting between buildings with frantic urgency—something short and hunched and fast...

"Did you see that?" she asked; already knowing they all had seen more than enough to confirm their worst fears. "They're out of control."

"We need to split up!" Lizzie called to the others, her voice taut with resolve. "They're going to come for Asher. We should try to draw them away."

Theo made a face but nodded reluctantly. "I'll cut around the block and see if I can find where they went."

"Simone—go with him," Lizzie instructed, her tone leaving no room for protest.

Simone hesitated, glancing at Asher. "You sure?"

"We'll be fine," Lizzie insisted as she grabbed Asher's hand and sprinted in the opposite direction—toward the old drive-in where it had all begun. As they ran, Lizzie clutched the shard of glass from her backpack—a fragile promise that their world was not so far from this one after all.

Theo and Simone hurried down a side street, Theo's breath coming in ragged gasps as he muttered something about needing a new cardio routine. The night was eerily still again, as if holding its breath in anticipation.

"I think we lost them," Theo said just as they turned another corner.

But Simone's eyes were wide with fear—and realization. "No," she replied urgently. "We didn't."

In an instant, the ground trembled beneath them once more—and another gaping hole appeared directly in their path. This time, it did not close immediately; instead, it yawned open with a menacing patience that sent chills down their spines.

Then: one by one—three figures emerged from its depths, each more grotesque than the last.

The first was squat and heavyset with thick limbs; its skin gleamed with plum-colored condensation beneath the streetlights as it sniffed the air like a feral beast on the hunt.

The second had long arms dragging nearly to the ground; eyes glowed like coals under heavy brows as it moved forward in determined strides.

The third was taller than either of its companions; its head smooth and featureless except for a single horizontal slit that opened into a mouth filled with jagged teeth. It let out a high-pitched screech when it saw them—a sound saturated by hunger and malice.

The Hollowkin advanced together, their movements twitchy but purposeful as they closed in on Theo and Simone.

"Run!" Theo shouted—but his feet felt glued to the pavement by terror or some unseen force binding him in place.

Simone grabbed his arm and pulled hard until momentum took over—dragging him along just steps ahead of their pursuers' reach. They charged up the block with adrenaline pumping furiously through their veins until another corner offered temporary sanctuary behind an old warehouse.

Panting heavily, Theo pressed his back against the building's cold brick wall while he caught his breath. "How do we stop those things?" he asked desperately between gasps.

Simone shook her head in disbelief but didn't hesitate: "I don't know—but we need bait."

Theo frowned—but then understanding dawned alongside fear and reluctance on his face.

"Don't use me for bait! I am not bait!" he protested weakly even as they both took off again—heading back toward Quarry Lane where more light—and more chances of escape—awaited them.

But as they rounded the corner the Hollowkin leapt out, surrounding them, hungry eyes ready to feast.

Theo was in the middle of a full blown panic attack when bright light erupted around them, engulfing the Hollowkin. The Hollowkin's awful screams pierced the night, sounding a lot like rabid cat's wailing in the dark, as the beams engulfed them. When the light died, the Hollowkin were no more.

Simone and Theo looked around frantically until their gaze came to rest on their rescuers. Asher's hands were still glowing as Lizzie smirked proudly, giving Asher a light punch to the shoulder. "Told ya it would work!"

"Were we bait?" Simone demanded in a stutter.

Theo just shook his head in disbelief, "doesn't feel good, does it? Wait, why are his hands glowing? What's inside Asher?"

"I'll explain later," Lizzie said dismissively, "right now we gotta get home. Who knows how many of those things are out here."

As they hustled off into the night, a new shadow peered at them from deep in the sinkhole.

"Soon," it hissed, "very soon."

Chapter 10: Break Line

The Friday before Spring Break bore all the familiar trademarks of a typical day at Southridge: the cafeteria served its predictably lukewarm lasagna, gym class was a whirlwind of chaos, and students had mentally checked out forty-eight hours prior. Dreams of sun-soaked beach trips, marathon video game sessions, and indulgent sleep-til-noon plans drifted through the corridors like pollen carried on a gentle, warm breeze.

Yet, for Lizzie Marlowe, "normal" ceased to exist the moment she had stepped through a slanted hole in the earth, entering a world filled with ethereal glowing trees, ancient floating ruins, and eerie doppelgängers. She sat at their usual lunch table, her gaze fixed on the shimmering glyph shard resting in her palm. It emitted a soft glow—faint yet persistent, pulsing rhythmically like a heartbeat that didn't belong to her.

Simone dropped into the seat across from her, a bag of jalapeño chips in hand and a mischievous smirk playing on her lips. "Let me guess. That ancient magical paperweight is acting up again?"

Lizzie nodded, her eyes never leaving the shard. "It's worse today. Every time I get near the gym, the pulsing intensifies."

"Maybe it just has a vendetta against dodgeball," Theo suggested, sliding into the seat beside Simone with a grin. "Like any rational person would."

Asher arrived last, moving quietly as usual, his silver eyes instinctively drawn to the shard even before he settled into his seat. "There's a sinkhole forming beneath the field house."

Lizzie blinked, caught off guard. "You sensed that?"

"I heard it," he replied, his voice barely above a whisper. "In my sleep. A whisper. Calling my name."

The table fell into a heavy silence, the normalcy of the day—sunlight streaming through high windows, the distant clatter of lunch trays—dissolving into a hazy, static background.

Then Lizzie stood, her voice steady and resolute. "We go back tonight."

Simone nearly choked on a chip, eyes wide with disbelief. "Wait—tonight tonight?"

Theo glanced around cautiously before leaning in closer. "Back to Acherra? You really think the real Asher's still alive?"

"I know he is," Lizzie affirmed, her voice filled with conviction. "We find him, we stop this thing from spiraling out of control. The Hollowkin, the Ascension, the strange glitches between here and there—it all traces back to him."

Asher nodded slowly, his expression thoughtful. "He's a part of me. I can feel it."

Simone groaned, a dramatic roll of her eyes, but there was no true objection. "Fine. But if I end up getting impaled by some mirror monster, I'm definitely haunting you."

That Night

The four of them met behind the Crestline Drive-In just after midnight, hoods up and flashlights off. The stars were dimmed by a crawling mist that didn't belong to any natural weather pattern. It curled across the lot like searching fingers.

"Ugh," Simone muttered, rubbing her arms. "I feel like I just walked into a ghost's armpit."

Theo adjusted the duffel bag slung over his shoulder. "Flashlights, snacks, extra batteries, and a crowbar. Because I refuse to get eaten without a fight."

"Are we sure this is a good idea? I mean, I know it's a BAD idea, but are we sure we should be doing this because it never works out," Simone told Lizzie as they checked and double-checker their supplies.

It hadn't been easy getting out of this house for any of them. They had to match each other's stories which ended up with them all having a sleepover at Asher's house. Getting Asher's fake parents to sound human was a challenge in itself and also blew the whole mission before it could even begin.

Lizzie shook her head in amusement thinking about it.

"Simone, Lizzie, and Theo are fine," Mr. Quinn had insisted over the phone, his voice flat and tinny as it reverberated through the receiver. "They are having fun."

"Yes," Mrs. Quinn added, her tone precisely synchronized if not awkwardly harmonious. "We have provisioned them with popcorn and movies. They are not engaged in any odd predicaments."

Lizzie's mom, on the other end of the line, sounded unconvinced. "Are you sure? Someone said she heard police cars earlier."

"There is no cause for alarm," Mr. Quinn replied briskly. "We have provided each child with adequate safety equipment."

"What does that mean?" Lizzie's mom asked.

"Helmets," Mrs. Quinn responded after a brief but noticeable pause, "and other human comforts like... pillows."

"Human comforts?" Lizzie's mom echoed, not sure if she had heard that right. Lizzie, for her part, slumped against the wall, shaking her head, this was a disaster.

"We also have marshmallows," Mr. Quinn interjected, as if suddenly remembering a critical component of human bonding rituals.

Lizzie's dad could be heard in the background asking if things were okay, to which her mom replied with audible skepticism, "I think so? They mentioned helmets and marshmallows?"

"The good ole days," Lizzie's dad could be heard reminiscing in the background.

A hurried whisper followed before Lizzie's mom returned to the call with renewed fervor. "If there's any trouble—"

"We will notify you immediately," the Quinns responded in perfect digital unison before hanging up with a mechanical click.

The line went dead for a moment before Theo's parents called with similar concerns.

"This is an automated message—" Mr. Quinn began, then quickly corrected himself, "I mean, this is Theo's friend's dad."

Theo's mother sounded perplexed. "Hello? Is anyone there?"

"We are enthusiastic to report that your child is alive," Mrs. Quinn chimed in with what was meant to be warmth but came out more like a warranty notice. "He is consuming sugar."

"Sugar?" Theo's mother asked suspiciously. "You know he gets hyper when he eats sugar—"

"Correct," Mr. Quinn replied swiftly. "He has been bouncing enthusiastically in a manner consistent with teenage behavior."

"Oh dear," Theo's mother sighed heavily over the line but seemed somewhat relieved by their attempt at reassurance.

Simone's parents were next.

"Can we talk to Simone?" her father demanded without preamble.

"She is occupied with activities appropriate for her age group!" Mrs. Quinn declared.

Simone's mother cut in anxiously: "Is she safe?"

"She has not yet broken any limbs or experienced existential crises," Mr. Quinn assured them after a brief pause suggested he was scanning through the list of possibilities.

"And you're watching them closely?" Simone's father pressed.

"With many eyes," they both confirmed simultaneously.

Simone snatched the phone quickly. "Mom, I'm fine. We are having a blast. It's…different."

Her mother wasn't skeptical. "Are you sure? What's the safe word?"

"Mom, oh my god!" Simone shouted, turning several shades of red.

"Safe word, young lady, or you're coming home."

Simone sighed into the phone and tried to cover her mouth as she spoke. "Bootsie," she finally ground out, causing Theo's eyes to widen in glee. A glare from Simone told him it was in his best interest to stay quiet.

"Have a great time, dear."

"Bye, mom," Simone huffed, hanging up the phone, embarrassed beyond words.

The three families exchanged bemused looks at their respective ends while Asher observed his own "parents" clicking into further standby mode—a testament to their unmatched ability to sound both almost-human and terribly unconvincing.

Now they stood together at the entrance of Acherra once more—the tilted hole behind the drive-in beckoning like gravity itself had reversed its pull.

"You really think this will work?" Theo asked nervously as they prepared to descend.

"It has to," Lizzie replied resolved.

Asher stood at the precipice of the collapsed concession stand, where the ground still sloped inward like a vast, ancient drainpipe leading to the gods. The air was thick with dust and anticipation. In Lizzie's hand, the glyph shard pulsed with an intense urgency, glowing so brightly that it cast long, flickering shadows across the debris-strewn ground.

"Time to go," Lizzie said, her voice unwavering and resolute, cutting through the tense silence.

Asher knelt and placed his hand gently on the cool, gritty earth. "Acherra," he whispered, his voice barely audible yet filled with purpose.

As if in response, the tunnel widened, its dark maw expanding and swallowing all sound as the slanted entrance yawned open to accept them once more. The shadows danced wildly, then settled as each of them, one by one, slid into the enveloping darkness, leaving the world above behind.

The Descent

The passage was different this time. No longer the soft-glass tunnel of Lizzie's first journey, this stretch of the slanted pathway throbbed with faint heat and sound—like moving through the throat of a sleeping beast.

The walls pulsed with brighter veins of green and violet light. Glyphs flickered in and out of sight like fireflies trapped beneath skin.

Theo muttered behind them, "Pretty sure this is how alien abductions start."

Simone gave him a light shove. "Too late to back out now, X-Files."

After what felt like miles of sloping travel, the tunnel rippled—and they stepped through the veil.

Lizzie gasped at the transformation of the world around them. The vast cavern they had entered before was now a pulsating network of tunnels, each branching off into its own labyrinthine path. The air shimmered with a heat that sent mirage-like ripples through the space, bending light and altering their perception. Lizzie felt as if she were inside a kaleidoscope, with colors shifting and bleeding into one another with every step.

Even the ground beneath them seemed to come alive—no longer just carpeted in soft grass, but now threaded with vivid veins of color that pulsed like arteries carrying light instead of blood. Small creatures scurried around them, their bodies flickering as though caught between dimensions, unable to decide which form to take.

"It's different," Lizzie breathed, her voice filled with awe and a hint of fear.

Asher nodded, his expression one of knowing acceptance. "It's always changing. Acherra is never the same twice."

Simone looked around, eyes wide with amazement. "It's like walking through a Lite Brite on acid."

"It feels unstable," Theo said nervously, glancing over his shoulder as if expecting something to leap out at them.

Asher's voice was calm but edged with urgency. "The Hollowkin are here somewhere. We have to keep moving."

They pressed on through the maze-like expanse where walls shifted unpredictably and pathways appeared to bend back on themselves. Every turn revealed new shapes and colors—translucent trees that vibrated with inner life, stones that floated lazily in midair, shedding pale fluorescent dust as they rotated.

Suddenly, the tranquil hum around them changed—a low rumble rose from deep within the tunnels, accompanied by a chorus of shrill cries that echoed ominously in the cavernous space.

"Them!" Asher shouted as dark forms emerged ahead—a group of Hollowkin clawing their way up from deeper levels, moving with frantic desperation toward the surface.

Lizzie felt panic swell within her. These were not like the single creature they had encountered before; there were many—too many—all advancing rapidly in a chaotic swarm.

"What do we do?" Simone yelled over the din, her voice tinged with both fear and defiance.

"Through here!" Asher gestured toward another tunnel—a narrow passageway barely visible behind glowing vines that twisted together like living filaments.

With no time to hesitate, they ducked into the passage just as three Hollowkin reached their previous spot—one squat and brutish with an awful beard trailing behind it like tangled wire; one tall and spindly with elongated limbs; and another bulbous and glistening slickly in the dim light.

The creatures let out furious shrieks when they realized their prey had slipped away—the sound tearing through air thickened by tension.

"Hurry!" Lizzie urged as they sprinted down the new path—its twists and turns disorienting but offering hope for escape.

The walls closed in around them until it felt more like crawling through an old ventilation shaft than traversing an ancient world—but still they pushed forward until at last—

They burst into open space again—a colossal chamber that stretched endlessly above and below, filled with floating structures orbiting like forgotten planets in a celestial dance.

Theo stared wide-eyed at the surreal vista before him, realizing that Lizzie's description of the place hadn't done it justice. To be honest, until that very moment, he still harbored doubts, wondering if Lizzie might have been experiencing a psychotic break and fabricating everything.

Above them, the cavern stretched infinitely, resembling the sky itself, illuminated from within by distant crystalline constellations that twinkled like stars from a forgotten galaxy. The floating ruins hovered overhead, rotating like ancient moons caught in a cosmic dance. The stone hand that Lizzie remembered still reached skyward in the distance, its orbiting glyphs now glowing with an intensity brighter than ever before.

But now… something had undeniably changed.

The colors were transformed—sharper and more vivid, with hues that seemed to penetrate the soul. In the distance, the white-glass trees stood shimmering with an eerie, unnatural stillness, their surfaces reflecting an ethereal glow.

Asher took a cautious step forward, and the ground beneath them pulsed in response, as if acknowledging their presence.

"They know we're here," he said, his voice tinged with a mixture of awe and trepidation.

"Who's 'they'?" Theo asked, clutching the crowbar with a grip so tight it might as well have been a lightsaber.

"Everyone," Lizzie whispered, her voice barely more than a breath. "Everything."

From deep within the woods, a howl echoed—a low, bone-rattling sound that felt dangerously close.

Lizzie turned toward the sound, her eyes blazing with determination and resolve.

"Let's go find the real Asher Quinn," she said, her voice steady and unwavering.

And with that, they ran, their footsteps echoing through the cavernous expanse as they plunged into the unknown.

Chapter 11: The Mirror Corridor

Acherra had always been a realm of restless energy, but here—deep beneath the shimmering crystal canopy and through the narrowing ravine of black-veined stone—the world seemed to thrum with a more deliberate intensity. It was as if the very air was charged with an unseen vigilance, watching their every move.

They arrived as if by accident, like wanderers who had stumbled onto sacred and forbidden ground. Before them stood a circular stone gate, seamlessly embedded in the rugged rock wall. Its edges were adorned with intricate glyphs, their carvings alive with a mystical shimmer, shifting between states—first solid, then transforming into ethereal smoke, and finally, glowing with a radiant light. At the gate's center, a curtain of silvery liquid undulated like a vertical pool, its surface alive with ripples that sang softly with a frequency so subtle yet potent that it sent shivers up their spines and made the hairs on their arms stand on end.

Asher stepped forward first, a sense of awe mixed with caution in his expression. "This is the Mirror Corridor," he announced, his voice barely above a whisper.

Theo arched an eyebrow, skepticism lacing his words. "That name doesn't exactly promise a 'friendly stroll.'"

"It's not meant to," Asher replied, his tone grave. "It's a reflection field. Within, we'll encounter echoes—versions of ourselves that could have been, or perhaps those that still might be."

Simone caught her reflection in the silvery veil, a fleeting glimpse of herself woven into the fabric of possibility. She turned back to the group with a smirk. "Well, if I come face-to-face with me and I have bangs, I'm running the other direction."

With a mix of brLizziedo and curiosity, she stepped through the shimmering veil, her form dissolving into its silvery depths. One by one, drawn by the pull of the unknown, they followed her into the enigmatic corridor.

The Corridor

The tunnel stretched endlessly before them, a surreal corridor of shimmering obsidian that seemed to defy the laws of nature. Its glossy walls mirrored not the travelers but distorted echoes of some otherworldly realm. Each step taken down this enigmatic passageway transformed the surroundings: light bent and refracted into kaleidoscopic patterns, sounds became muffled whispers, and time itself seemed to coil into a disorienting lull. They moved in a solemn procession, one after the other, as the silence wrapped around them like an ever-tightening shroud. And then, the strangeness escalated.

Simone's Reflections

Simone was the first to slow her pace, her footsteps faltering as the wall beside her began to shimmer with an otherworldly glow, irresistibly drawing her gaze. Her reflection in the gleaming surface fractured into three distinct versions of herself, each more vivid than the last.

The first Simone stood proudly, enveloped in a regal coat of lustrous black feathers that caught the light with a mesmerizing sheen. Her eyes blazed with a fierce golden fire, casting an intense glow across a battlefield that crackled with arcs of lightning. Her voice resonated from the mirror with the power of thunder, proclaiming, "I burn before I break."

The second version of Simone sat serenely cross-legged in a dimly lit library, the warm glow of countless candles casting flickering shadows around her. Intricate tattoos wound their way up her arms, shifting and twisting like living glyphs. She read from a scroll that floated before her, her voice a rhythmic chant. Around her, stones hovered gracefully in the air, and ethereal fox-creatures flickered into being, their forms shimmering in the candlelight.

The third Simone, however, was a haunting specter of silence. She trembled, her skin ashen and fractured like parched earth. Her eyes were absent, replaced by hollow, cavernous sockets that seemed to gaze into infinity. Her mouth opened, releasing a cascade of black sand that spilled onto the mirrored floor, a dark river against the gleaming surface.

Simone recoiled in horror, stepping back abruptly. "Nope. Not dealing with creepy cryptkeeper me today," she declared, shaking off the unsettling vision with a shudder.

Theo's Reflections

Theo halted after a few paces, his gaze catching on his reflection. It didn't shimmer as reflections normally do; instead, it flickered erratically, like the distorted images of a worn-out VHS tape.

In the first vision, he appeared as a hooded tech-sLizzient, surrounded by an array of holographic screens hovering in the air. Each screen was alive with the faces of hundreds, a digital sea of expressions. His fingers danced across a keyboard, typing in a complex glyph-code at a speed beyond human perception, effortlessly rewiring a colossal and perilous system with nothing more than sheer instinct and a sharp wit.

The second vision showed him standing atop a tower constructed entirely from bones, his eyes glowing an eerie white. Intricate glyphs were etched into his skin, resembling a complex network of circuitry. With a commanding presence, he raised a staff high above his head, controlling the Hollowkin as if they were mere marionettes under his spell.

In the third vision, he was bound to a gnarled tree, chained and whispering apologies into the earth. His form flickered like a faulty bulb, unstable and on the verge of fading into oblivion.

Theo frowned deeply, contemplating the unsettling scenes. "Okay... I kinda want to be the hacker-me. But not the tree-me. That dude is having a really bad day."

Asher's Reflections

Asher hesitated as he neared the bend in the corridor, where the walls were now fractured with mirrored blue crystal veins. His reflections were unsettlingly vivid—they didn't just shimmer or glitch—they cried out in silent agony.

The first Asher was the surface-world Asher—real, original, yet imprisoned within a translucent barrier. His hands pounded desperately against the walls, his mouth forming a soundless scream. His eyes were locked on Asher, filled with a silent plea for help.

The second reflection was even more haunting. It was Asher—but transformed into a Hollowkin. His features were distorted, his mouth grotesque and wrong, with eyes like empty pits of ash. He reached through the mirror, claws etching deep marks into the wall, whispering, "Let me in."

The third reflection was a disturbing amalgamation. A version of Asher... merged. He was perfectly balanced, his skin glinting like Acherra stone, and his silver eyes serene. He stood on floating ruins, manipulating light and shadow with the poise of a living glyph.

Asher stumbled back, his breath quickening, caught between fear and fascination.

"Is that... me?" he questioned, his voice thick with doubt. "Is that who I become?"

Lizzie silently took his hand, offering comfort without answers.

Lizzie's Reflections

Then the corridor warped violently once more—and Lizzie's moment arrived with a menacing chill in the air.

Her first reflection was a scene of chaos: she stood before the Crestline Drive-In, her hands ablaze with an unnatural glow, as the sky above shattered like a pane of glass. Her voice thundered in accusation: "You opened it. You made the choice."

The second vision was even more bizarre. Lizzie found herself on a shoreline of liquid light, her arms marked with intricate glyphs, and beside her, her mother—youthful, with eyes glowing like embers. Her mother's words were a silent whisper, lost to Lizzie, before she thrust a glowing shard into Lizzie's chest with an urgency that left Lizzie breathless.

The third Lizzie was an unrecognizable warrior, encased in armor, her eyes replaced by an eerie, solid silver gleam. She marched through a devastated Southridge, her voice an emotionless drone: "There is no merge. There is only the tear."

Without warning, a fourth Lizzie materialized, her visage twisted and haunted, staring deep into Lizzie's soul with an intensity that chilled her to the core: "You are not who you appear to be. Be mindful. The world about you is wrong."

A violent shiver coursed through Lizzie, shaking her to her very bones. Her neck tingled with a creeping dread down her spine. "What did that mean," she thought in terror, "I'm not who I appear to be?"

The corridor convulsed.

Lizzie's shard, gripped tightly in her hand, throbbed with a blistering, searing heat.

Then the corridor constricted brutally, leading to a dead end—a massive glyph lock pulsating with fractured, sinister symbols.

The Lock

The group stood in awe before the massive door that barred their way, its imposing presence casting long shadows across the stone floor. "What do we do now?" Theo asked, his voice tinged with surprise and uncertainty.

"I don't know," Asher responded, his brow furrowed in confusion, "I've never seen this before."

"You've never seen it?" Theo retorted, disbelief coloring his tone.

"No, never," Asher replied, equally shocked, "and I've crossed this area many times."

Suspended in midair before them was a circular frame that spun with a deliberate grace, composed of interlocking rings etched with glowing runes. Some of these symbols were familiar, whispering of ancient tales, while others were alien, their meanings obscured by time. At the center of this intricate mechanism floated a dark glass core, cracked and trembling as if with anticipation.

"It's broken," Simone observed, her eyes narrowing as she studied the damaged core.

"No," Lizzie whispered, her voice barely audible over the hum of the runes. "It's waiting."

With a determined step forward, Lizzie extended her hand, revealing a shard that seemed to pulse with its own light. As she approached, the lock responded, flaring brilliantly as if awakening from a long slumber. The shard leapt from her hand with a life of its own, snapping into the core of the lock with a resonant finality.

The symbols spun wildly, a blur of luminescence, before clicking into place with a deep, resonant clang that echoed through the corridor. The mirrored walls shivered and rippled as if alive, then slowly sank away, revealing a doorway that led not into another dark tunnel, but into a realm bathed in light.

A warm, humming glow greeted them, carrying a scent that was both strange and familiar, like burnt air mingled with the soothing fragrance of lavender.

Asher hesitated, stepping forward cautiously. "This was sealed for a reason," he murmured, the weight of history heavy in his words.

"And we're opening it anyway," Lizzie said, her smile grim but resolute.

Together, hearts pounding with the thrill of the unknown, they stepped through the door and into the light beyond.

Long after Lizzie, Asher, Simone, and Theo had crossed through the glyph-etched doorway into uncharted realms, the Mirror Corridor refused to yield to silence. Its myriad reflections continued to glisten under a ghostly light, shifting and shimmering with an almost sentient vibrancy. Deep within the corridor's endless expanse of impenetrable obsidian, far beyond any solitary reflection and nestled in the dancing fissures of unpredictable possibility, something began to stir.

It was neither a creature of Acherra nor one of the Hollowkin; it was something far older, emerging from a corner of the corridor so deep and polished it seemed untouched by time. Out of the gloom, a shadow slowly coalesced into sharp focus—a mere suggestion of form rather than a complete entity. This was a reflection that defied its source, the distorted silhouette of a tall figure whose limbs stretched like wet ink bleeding on darkened canvas. Its eyes, if they could be called that, appeared as twin voids—emptiness that paradoxically shimmered with an unsettling awareness.

In that silent vigil, it had observed every detail: it watched as Lizzie clutched her glowing shard, observed Asher bathed in a subtle luminescence, noted Theo's clever and uncertain maneuvers, and detected Simone's wild yet crystalline clarity. And with every observation, a faint, knowing smile played upon its enigmatic countenance.

Behind this imposing figure, other reflections quivered into existence—faint and obscured, like errant silhouettes on a dimly lit stage, pacing with constrained yet restless energy.

One of these apparitions wore an ancient crown forged from shattered glyphs that sparkled like broken constellations. Another writhed in a mesmerizing dance, its limbs dissolving and reforming like tendrils of smoke in a shifting breeze. A third, utterly faceless, presented only a vacant mirror that ominously reflected the hidden fears of all who glanced upon it.

The tall figure advanced deliberately toward the mirror that Lizzie had once touched—a mirror on which her own reflection had chillingly cautioned, "You are not who you appear to be." As it neared, it gently pressed a hand, comprised of long, glass-thin fingers, against the cool, undulating surface. Instantly, a ripple spread across the mirror like a stone cast in still water, distorting every visage, every timeline, and every potentiality it contained.

When its voice finally broke through the quiet, it echoed hauntingly, much like wind coursing through the shattered arches of an ancient cathedral. "The Veil has thinned. The echoes awaken. The Glyphtorn remembers," it intoned, each syllable laden with foreboding power.

Almost immediately, another voice emerged from the enveloping darkness—ragged and whispering like shredded parchment flapping in a violent storm. "And the shard has chosen a vessel."

The faceless entity leaned closer, causing the mirror to twist and warp in response to its looming presence. "She is incomplete. She will fail," it declared in a tone that dripped with icy certainty.

A hushed counter replied from the mysterious tall figure, its voice as calm and resolute as the final note of a long-forgotten hymn. "No, she will try. And that is all we need."

From somewhere deep within the maze-like, fragmented walls of the corridor, a sound akin to ancient stone groaning as it was dragged across brittle bone resonated—a lament of something primordial awakening. A thousand reflections trembled in perfunctory unison as the very air seemed to vibrate with a mysterious, impending force.

Then, building in intensity, the tall figure spoke once again, this time its voice booming with authority so that every echo in the corridor could feel its presence: "The Ascension is upon us. Prepare the corridors. Let the Hollowkin feed. We open the Gate soon."

A powerful pulse reverberated along the corridor—once, twice—like the relentless beating of a drum signaling the impending end of all things. And in that heavy, charged moment, the shifting reflections stilled to silence. The mirror, as if living and devouring, swallowed the silent watchers whole, leaving behind only the residue of its unfathomable mystery.

Chapter 12: The Real One

The light from the glyph door dimmed and dissolved behind them like the gentle exhale of a long-forgotten sigh, giving way to a soft, radiant glow that pulsed in rhythm with an almost tangible heartbeat. Beyond lay a vast chamber, its width and tranquil majesty speaking of ages past— a place older, quieter, and infinitely more mysterious than any corner of Acherra they had ever encountered.

This hall was not sculpted from cold, unyielding crystal but from the very essence of memory itself. The walls were flanked by grand columns, each one intricately etched with glyphs that writhed and morphed like living streams of thought, their patterns fluid and mesmerizing. Overhead, the ceiling arched in a dome of shimmering glass that captured and refracted the light into drifting auroras, painting the space with colors of otherworldly wonder. At the heart of this surreal chamber, cradled in a bed of ancient stone and swirling mist, lay a boy.

He rested curled on his side, appearing to be in a deep slumber—yet even from afar, a deep and instinctive recognition stirred within Lizzie. "Asher?" she whispered, as if the sound of his name could bridge the cosmic distance.

At her call, the boy stirred. Slowly, agonizingly, as if each movement was a battle against an unseen force. His skin, ghostly pale, did not merely reflect a lack of color but exuded a presence as if the light of life was being gradually siphoned from him. His soft brown hair—longer and more entangled than the Asher she remembered—brushed against his face with sleepy disarray. And as his eyes fluttered open, they revealed a depth of humanity interwoven with a fierce recognition that transcended time.

Nearby, the other Asher— the one who had journeyed with them—stopped dead in his tracks, his jaw slack in disbelief. It was as if two mirrors, each reflecting a half-forgotten truth, had suddenly met and blinked in mutual astonishment.

The boy in the stone cradle slowly sat up, his voice emerging as a fragile whisper that seemed to echo from deep underground. "Are... you me?" he inquired, the words laden with a tremor of both hope and sorrow.

The traveling Asher hesitated, stepping forward with trembling hands. "I think... I was meant to be," he murmured, his voice caught between wonder and despair.

Lizzie's heart constricted painfully as the pair of boys regarded one another like estranged twins finally reunited, their connection resonating far beyond mere resemblance. It was as though their very beings vibrated in harmony; from beneath their skin a faint silver luminescence pooled, outlining their veins like celestial maps—stars reclaiming their ancient constellations.

In that charged moment, the very chamber pulsed, and a new presence arrived with the weight of inevitability. "Do not touch!" boomed a voice that resonated throughout the expansive space.

Meridra emerged from the luminous glow as if she had always been its living embodiment. Her robes flowed around her like liquid dusk, iridescent and mesmerizing, while her face bore the solemn lines of a timeless guardian. Yet her eyes shimmered with a gentle, aching pain that belied her calm exterior.

Both versions of Asher turned in unison. The surface Asher, his head tilting in a gesture of reverence and recognition, uttered, "I remember you... You came to me in my dreams, countless times."

With a graceful motion, Meridra knelt between the two boys, her voice soft and mournful—a lullaby woven with loss as she spoke, "My sons."

Simone's jaw dropped in astonishment. "Wait. What?"

A quiet murmur from Theo punctuated the air with a wry, "Plot twist."

In a hushed, yet resolute tone, Lizzie asked, "I... what do you mean?" even as a part of her had anticipated this revelation.

Meridra stretched out her hand toward both boys, though her fingers hovered without making contact. "I am of Acherra—a former Keeper of Memory, now transformed into something else entirely: Asher's mother. My child was born here, yet he was never made whole. His soul was fragmented long ago, an act that ignited the enigmatic

Merge. We do not yet understand the precise mechanics of this occurrence; we only know that once it begins, each fractured half must be reconciled. His twin spark existed Above, and the sole path to salvation for both was to complete that sacred Merge."

"You look like my mother," the Above Asher said quietly, a mixture of hope and uncertainty in his voice.

Meridra gave him a sympathetic smile, "I am, and I am not, just as my Asher is you and yet he isn't."

"My mother..." he began, his eyes brimming with sadness and longing.

"...was lost long ago. But I am here, Asher. And as she loved you, so shall I," she smiled at him, her warmth tinged with the weight of something unsaid.

"But how can you," he asked, his voice cracking, carrying years of sorrow and doubt.

Meridra finally drew him into a comforting embrace, though her own heart ached with the complexity of it all. "Because I am her as much as you are my Asher, there is a bond there. Her love for you resides in me. And even without that knowledge, I would know you are mine."

Above Asher hugged her back, holding tight as if afraid she might vanish. Meridra then turned to Acherra Asher, whose eyes shimmered with unshed tears, caught between joy and lingering disbelief.

"Mother..."

Meridra gently brushed the hair from his face and placed a finger on either side of his temple. "Remember, my son." A light pulsed where she touched, and Acherra Asher's eyes clouded before shining brightly, as if he was piecing together a fragmented past.

Acherra Asher blinked several times, looking at Meridra as if truly seeing her for the first time. "Mom?" he asked, his voice a tapestry of hope and hesitation.

"Hello, love," she smiled at him, though her heart fluttered with the weight of the moment.

"Mom!" he shouted, joy overpowering any remnants of doubt as he rushed into her embrace.

Lizzie, Simone, and Theo turned away, overwhelmed by the raw emotion of the reunion, each grappling with their own feelings.

But the beautiful moment was fleeting, as Meridra addressed them all with a heavy heart. "Boys, we have to merge you. If not, neither will survive. Do you understand?"

Both Ashers nodded, though the knowledge of the truth was tangled with fear and uncertainty about what such a union would mean for them.

Theo raised his hand slowly, as if mimicking a question from an old classroom lecture. "Okay, but how exactly does that work? Is it like magic? A twist of genetics? Perhaps a clone situation? Because I once read something about CRISPR and—"

"They are not clones, young one," Meridra interjected gently, "but rather, they are akin to twins. This is ancient magic—older than any realm you know. Born from the very first fracture of the mirror realms, his essence was split between Above and Below, forming two distinct beings that share one true soul. If they Merge willingly, they become a whole that is far stronger than any single fragment."

Lizzie turned to the weary, luminous Asher from Acherra, her voice heavy with concern. "Then what occurred? Why did the Merge fail?"

Meridra's eyes darkened with resignation. "The Ascension."

A thick silence unfurled across the chamber like a heavy curtain dropped in slow motion.

"Okay, really," Simone protested, "can we stop pretending we understand what that is? It sounds like some sort of apocalyptic yoga session."

"The Ascension," Meridra continued, her tone measured and grave, "is the enforced merging of Acherra and the surface world—not merely of people but of time, memory, and form. What was once a sacred prophecy has been tainted by corruption, now desperately seeking unity through a process of collapse."

Theo frowned, trying to simplify the enormity of it. "It's like forcing two puzzle pieces together that no longer fit."

"Exactly," Meridra confirmed. "It is unraveling the veil between the worlds. Amid that chaos, Asher's mind became a refuge—it suppressed the unfolding truth to protect him, leaving him to wander the surface as if he were only half his soul. The two worlds, long separated and yet inexplicably linked, continued their independent yet intertwined existence."

Clutching his arms as if to hold himself together, Surface Asher murmured, "That's why I always felt... off, like I wasn't truly at home in my own skin."

"You didn't," whispered the Acherra Asher, his tone filled with soft empathy. "Neither did I."

Once more, the two boys exchanged an intense, silent gaze as a palpable pull surged between them, their inner glow intensifying to a brightness that outshone any glyph or shard. But just as their connection neared its breakthrough, Meridra intervened, her hand raised in gentle denial. "No. Not yet."

Both boys blinked, their minds reeling in disorientation. "The Merge must be willing," she explained softly, "and complete. If rushed... it will shatter you. There remains in each of you unhealed pain and fear. You must prepare yourselves."

Stepping between the two, Lizzie asked with determined resolve, "So what do we do? How can we halt the Ascension?"

Meridra turned slowly to face her, an enigmatic smile tugging at the corners of her expression. "You already hold a piece of the answer," she said, nodding toward the shimmering shard tucked in Lizzie's pocket.

Simone exhaled sharply, half-amused and half-overwhelmed. "Well, that's comforting. An ancient, world-ending prophecy, and our salvation hinges on a glowing rock and a couple of magic twins."

Theo glanced between the two Ashers, his curiosity unabashed. "So... if they Merge, does one simply disappear? Or does it become some supercharged fusion? Do we end up with a Mega Asher?"

The Above Asher raised an eyebrow with quiet exasperation, "You're not making this any easier."

With a shrug, Theo replied, "I think I am helping. We have to keep our humor even as we face the end of everything we know."

Acherra Asher managed a weak smile. "I kind of like him," he murmured.

Asher from Above nodded in agreement. "Same."

Lizzie looked between the two, her expression soft yet filled with unwavering determination. "Then we proceed together. One step at a time. Whatever the Merge signifies—whatever destiny the Ascension has in store—we face it as one."

In a moment of serene inevitability, the two Ashers exchanged a look heavy with unspoken promises. As if drawn by a force beyond comprehension, each reached out for the other's hand—but they did not touch, not yet.

Their gentle radiance grew in intensity, a luminous glow brighter than any glyph or mystical shard could ever be.

And far away, in the shadowed recesses of Acherra where reflections reigned and ancient corridors whispered secrets, a dozen mirrors began to fracture, their delicate surfaces cracking in silent, portentous admonition.

Chapter 13: The Ascension

The fading radiance of the sacred chamber receded like a distant memory as Meridra led the group through a narrow corridor hewn from living stone. Each step echoed on the soft, earthen floor, and the cool air carried a rich blend of scents—damp ancient roots entwined with the subtle, sweet aroma of luminous moss. For several long moments, silence reigned among them; even Theo's thoughts seemed to be hushed under the weight of the emotional tide left behind in the hall of the Real One, a tide as dense and lingering as the steam that rises after a torrential summer storm.

Lizzie moved in close beside the regal Above Asher, whose shoulder brushed hers ever so gently as if reassuring her with silent strokes of warmth. Trailing behind them was the other Asher—quiet in his resolve yet exuding a steady presence that anchored their collective spirit. Simone, her gaze fixed on Theo, stayed near him with her hand always poised at his elbow, a delicate guard against the fear she refused to admit even to herself.

They soon emerged into a space that felt like home—a vaulted sanctuary draped in cascading vines, nestled deeply within a fold of the crystalline forest. This was the sacred ground where Meridra had first appeared to Lizzie and the Ashers, where hidden truths had begun to unravel like intricately knotted threads. In this haven, the light pulsed with a slower, more deliberate rhythm, each beam exuding a gentle warmth. Nearby, ancient scrolls floated lazily in the air, and a muted waterfall tumbled down one wall into a basin that glowed with a calming, cerulean light.

"Here," Meridra intoned, her voice a low, steady cadence that resonated within the chamber. "You will rest. But not for long."

At her words, Asher—the one from the surface—collapsed onto the ground like a marionette whose strings had finally slackened. His double mirrored the descent with an eerie synchronicity. Theo sank beside them, his backpack finally abandoning its perch on his shoulders. Simone theatrically slumped against a weathered pillar, exhaling a long-held breath as if releasing the weight of unseen burdens.

"Okay, so... ancient magic twins, soul fusion, and me almost wetting myself. Any other surprises?" she quipped, a spark of ironic humor cutting through the tension.

Meridra's gentle smile held a secret promise, yet she said nothing in response. Instead, she reached out toward a shimmering pool at the center of the sanctuary. As her extended hand brushed the water, it rippled into life, rising into a veil of light that shimmered and danced with ethereal energy. Within this fluid curtain emerged visions of surreal calamities: cities folding in on themselves like paper origami, children vanishing mid-step as though erased by a mischievous hand, and adults wandering through disorienting, unfamiliar streets whose shadows carried the echo of forgotten dreams.

"The Ascension," she pronounced gravely, her voice a solemn bell tolling truth, "is no longer a mere prophecy. It has begun."

Drawn closer by the pull of destiny, Lizzie stepped forward, feeling the shard in her pocket pulse with an almost feverish heat. "Tell us everything," she requested, her voice trembling with both resolve and trepidation.

Meridra nodded solemnly. "The Ascension is the inexorable merging of Acherra and the Surface, a moment when all divisions collapse and every soul encounters its mirror image. Once, it was revered as sacred—a natural culmination of our shared evolution. But something has shifted, something—or someone—has intervened."

A hushed murmur passed through the group. "The Architect," Asher whispered, his voice barely audible.

"Yes," Meridra affirmed. "The Architect is an entity not born of magic, but of sheer manipulation. It is a being that contends the only viable path forward is one of forced unity. Its aim is to banish chaos through the imposition of control, to merge all beings at once, ignorant of whether they are truly ready for such a transformation."

Theo exhaled, heavy with disquiet. "But you said incomplete Merges could be lethal. Or even worse," he murmured.

"And that is precisely what is unfolding now," Meridra replied. "People are mutating, vanishing unexpectedly. Some exist in both realms yet no longer recognize their own reflection. Memories bleed into one another, time shatters into fragments, and reality trembles with relentless uncertainty."

Simone, her voice uncharacteristically somber, crossed her arms. "And no one is doing anything to stop it?"

"Some have tried, though many have failed," Meridra explained, her gaze sweeping over Lizzie and the Ashers. "But you—you are the bridge. Lizzie, your mother was among the first humans to undergo the Merge without even understanding it. Her mind persevered; her body adapted."

Lizzie's heart plummeted at the revelation. "My mom?" she echoed, shock mingled with disbelief.

Stepping closer, Meridra urged her to reflect. "Think back—those fragmented dreams, her mysterious disappearances, the cryptic symbols she would sketch in the night. She merged long ago, living evidence that such a transformation can occur safely, though never without profound sacrifice."

Lizzie staggered back, her thoughts a storm of recollections and unanswered questions—her mother's odd behavior, the riddles she had spoken in whispers, the uncanny way she seemed to read Lizzie's mind before a word was even spoken.

"But why her? Why wasn't it common among others?" Lizzie pressed, seeking clarity amidst the tumult.

"Her double in Acherra was predisposed, already attuned. A Keeper, like me—a spiritual bridge even before the

Merge. But now..." Meridra's voice trailed off as she turned once more toward the glowing pool.

Within the enchanted water, new visions emerged: sinkholes tearing through familiar neighborhoods, elusive Hollowkin skittering out from the cracks, mirrors that twisted and absorbed stray reflections as if devouring misaligned identities.

"The Architect is expediting this catastrophic process," Meridra continued. "He deploys the Hollowkin as his minions, scavenging for vulnerable souls and coercing them into merging—often with violent, unpredictable consequences."

Theo released a long, weary breath. "So... worst-case scenario: the entire world glitches like a broken video game."

"Yes," Meridra agreed with a measured nod. "That is the very outcome we must prevent, unless we can stop him."

Exchanging solemn glances, the two Ashers felt the soft glow between them intensify—a pulse of light resembling twin heartbeats echoing across an immense chasm.

"But then why isn't the world above overrun with the feats of superheroes and supervillains? How is it that nothing like that is ever reported?" Theo challenged, his tone half incredulous.

Meridra's smile held an enigmatic glimmer as she replied softly, "Oh, but you have noticed. Your surface history is teeming with such sightings, quickly reclassified as myth or fable to tame their edge."

"Such as...?" Theo prompted, his curiosity piqued.

"Vampires, werewolves, even figures like Hitler and Einstein—these forms are multitudinous. When the Merge goes awry, you witness terrifying horrors; when it is harmonious, heroes emerge, role models shine, and intellects and saints grace our midst. Yet, most choose to return, keeping their tempered lives anchored here in Acherra."

"Wait, wait, wait... vampires?!" Theo almost shouted, his astonishment palpable.

Meridra nodded slowly, her expression grave. "This is why the Merge cannot be taken lightly. And now, with the Architect preparing his final move, our actions must be swift and decisive."

"We need to locate his hiding place," Lizzie declared, her voice steadying as determination burned within her. "And stop the Ascension before the surface itself collapses."

"You must first find the Broken Citadel," Meridra instructed, her tone imbued with urgency. "It lies at the convergence of all fractures—a realm where the threads of time and identity unravel. There, the Architect readies his final act."

Lizzie turned to her comrades, her eyes a tempest of fear intertwined with unyielding fire. "Then that's where we go," she resolved.

In a shadowed chamber deep within Acherra—a room where mirrored walls rippled like liquid oil under unseen flames and eyes burned from the reflections—a presence watched. The Architect, formless yet all-pervasive, lingered with the weight of shifting geometry that bent space in eerie patterns. Every reflection lay exposed before it, every potential outcome etched into its being.

"They gather," the Architect intoned to the silent assembly behind the glass, its voice an omnipresent murmur. "The bridge forms. The shards realign."

As the mirrors trembled in reverent fear or anticipation, it declared in a voice that seethed with inevitability, "Let them come. The Ascension is no longer a matter of possibility—it is a destined, inescapable event."

And from the void, the Architect smiled, a gesture that promised both transformation and unsettling destiny.

It started with a faint, elusive flicker. In the dim glow of the Friday night gym, Southridge's weary janitor, Harold Mackey, wiped his tired eyes as he pushed a battered mop bucket along the ornate yet deserted corridor. The stale tang of ammonia mixed with the lingering odor of aged sweat, wrapping around him like a heavy, suffocating blanket. The building was swathed in an almost tangible silence, a quietude that echoed off the walls and was sporadically interrupted by the slow, methodical sloshing of murky water and the jittery pulse of fluorescent lights overhead.

Unbeknownst to him, a malevolent void was forming—a mysterious sinkhole in the middle of the hallway. At first, his focus was solely on his routine, and he failed to perceive the subtle disturbance beneath his feet. Then, in an eerie moment of stillness, the floor yielded without a sound, revealing a gaping spiral of glassy darkness that spread across the linoleum with a graceful, unnatural fluidity. Harold's attention snapped to it just in time to see his mop bucket tilt precariously over the edge, vanishing into the dark like a discarded pebble swallowed by an ancient well.

"What in the—" he murmured, startled, when movement erupted from the obscurity behind him. From the depths of the shadows came a series of rapid, skittering sounds—each wet, clicking noise slicing through the silence. Spinning around, his heart thundering in his chest, Harold's eyes swept the dim corridor, now hauntingly empty. His breath materialized as a frosted mist in the sudden, chilling drop in temperature.

Then, as if summoned by the darkness itself, a disembodied whisper slithered through the cold air: "He's unmerged..." In that moment, a dozen sinister, crimson eyes illuminated from hidden recesses, and the Hollowkin materialized as a single, nightmarish mass. They were a writhing tangle of spindly limbs and jagged claws, coated in slick, undulating skin and accented by impossibly wide mouths stretched in silent horror. Stumbling backwards in panic, Harold barely registered the relentless approach of the sinkhole that now loomed at his heels.

"Stay away!" he shouted, his voice trembling, as he fumbled along his belt for the radio. Yet, the Hollowkin made no immediate move to attack; instead, they encircled him as if performing an ominous ritual. One entity among them, larger and more imposing than its comrades, stepped forward from the clutch of shadow. Reaching out with a grotesquely twisted finger, it traced a chilling path to Harold's forehead. At that moment, a ripple of searing energy coursed through him—an abrupt, disorienting jolt that arched his back and transformed his scream into an otherworldly shriek that reverberated against the walls with an almost metallic sharpness.

The merging began. In the depths of his mind, Harold's vision fractured, revealing another version of himself—a man who had never taken the quiet janitorial job at Southridge but had instead joined the military, bearing the harsh scars of war and fire. Two starkly contrasting lives collided with a force reminiscent of tectonic plates grinding against each other; the impact twisted his body grotesquely, elongated his limbs unnaturally, and contorted his voice into a guttural growl that no longer seemed entirely human.

As the transformation progressed, Harold's skin split in places, unveiling glowing, arcane glyphs etched beneath— a constellation of symbols burning with a spectral, unnatural light. His once familiar brown eyes now pulsated with an erratic flicker, as if harboring a chaotic, flickering flame within. What began as a piercing scream rapidly degenerated into a fearsome roar that tore through the silence.

The Hollowkin watched this metamorphosis with an eerie, almost reverent glee. One rasped in a voice like brittle ice, "He is unbalanced... but useful." Now nearly unrecognizable, Harold—if he could still be called that—stumbled forward under the weight of his altered state. His jaw unhinged grotesquely, and from deep within, a resonant pulse of sound erupted, fracturing the windows around him with its sheer intensity. His hands morphed into sLizziege claws, scraping against the wall as he barreled towards the exit, forcefully shattering the doors before disappearing into the merciless embrace of the night.

One by one, the Hollowkin melted back into the darkness, their task complete as the once vibrant corridors of the school fell into a haunting, oppressive quiet once more. Yet far beyond the building's confines, a cacophony of distant screams began to swell, a grim harbinger of the night's unfolding chaos. The Ascension had claimed another soul, leaving only echoes of terror in its wake.

Chapter 14: The Shifting Town

The iridescent shimmer of Acherra clung to them like an otherworldly mist as the two Ashers stepped gingerly from the radiant tunnel and into the last fragile hues of twilight along Quarry Lane. The suburban landscape, once warmly familiar, now appeared strange and diminished—its houses flattened under a brittle veneer, as if a single misstep might send them crumbling into dust. The air was heavy and still; birds offered no song, and the elongated shadows on the pavement seemed to stretch with an eerie persistence while a faint taste of static lingered at the back of their throats.

They had returned to the surface world.

Asher—the one whose essence was born from the mysterious Acherra—took the lead, guiding his counterpart down the winding cul-de-sac. Their steps were measured as they approached the stark, clinical white house perched at the end of the street. At that precise moment, the porch light flickered into existence with uncanny precision, as if it were triggered by their very presence or perhaps by an inexorable cosmic inevitability. Before their trembling hands could reach out to knock, the front door whooshed open with a calculated, ghostly precision.

"Welcome home," intoned Mr. Quinn, his voice stiff and rehearsed, yet betraying an unsettling twitch, as though it were programmed to hide some unspoken anomaly.

"We have gladly updated the thermostat to a pleasing 72 degrees," Mrs. Quinn chimed in mechanically, her hands clasped in a practiced gesture of warmth and precision. "Would you like... toast?"

Both Ashers hesitated at the threshold, caught in a suspended moment of uncertainty. With a hesitant step forward, Acherra Asher broke the silence.

"Father... Mother... I've brought someone with me."

The robotic parents tilted their heads in eerie unison, their artificial eyes flickering with a subtle hint of digital awareness. For a heartbeat, Mrs. Quinn's practiced smile wavered as if caught between programmed glee and something closer to genuine surprise.

"This unit detects... duplicate presence," she announced brightly.

"This is not standard protocol," Mr. Quinn added in a measured tone, "Initiating... emotional approximation... protocol."

In unison, their hands clapped in an oddly mechanical jubilation.

"Congratulations! You are two now!" they declared jubilantly.

Surface Asher blinked in confused astonishment. "I... what?"

Mr. Quinn continued, patting the couch as if trying to usher in an awkward formality, "We had suspected that your return would involve... multiplicity. You are both valid, albeit slightly glitched, but unequivocally valid."

Moments later, Mrs. Quinn briskly made her way into the kitchen as though on autopilot. "We shall prepare double dinner. Two perfectly grilled cheeses. Four slices of golden bread. And sixteen whole units of affection," she declared in a tone that mixed artificial cheer with underlying surreality.

"Please do not Merge on the furniture," Mr. Quinn intoned gravely, his voice a stern contrast to the earlier cheerfulness.

The two Ashers exchanged glances that fluctuated between horror and helpless amusement, as if their very existence teetered on the edge of absurdity.

"Home sweet home," murmured Acherra Asher with a note of resignation.

"Yep," Surface Asher replied quietly, his voice heavy with incredulity. "Definitely weirder than I remembered."

Then erupted the cacophony of screams.

Mr. Quinn's head whipped toward the window with a rapid series of clattering clicks. "Neighborhood alert. Massive surge in dimensional instability!" he barked, his voice edged with urgency.

From outside came the deafening roar of warped time—buildings violently flickering in and out of existence, shadows cast crazily upward instead of down. The two Ashers bolted toward the front yard as Meridra's voice thundered from Acherra, resonating through the glyph shard in Surface Asher's pocket.

"Chaos is here," it declared ominously.

Suddenly, a gaping sinkhole exploded in the middle of the street, devouring a car parked along the curb with a crunching finality. Panic-stricken people scattered in all directions, a torrent of bodies fleeing for safety. Yet most unnerving of all—was the hysterical laughter.

A figure erupted from behind the neighbor's hedge, its skin a chaotic, flickering mass. A Hollowkin, grotesquely draped in the form of the high school janitor like a grotesque, oversized sweater, cackled maniacally as it lunged toward the Quinn house.

"Go, go, go!" Surface Asher shouted, adrenaline coursing through his veins.

They sprinted toward the alley, weaving through flickering stop signs and dodging a dumpster that grotesquely transformed into a glass coffin before snapping back to rusted metal.

"Behind the shed!" Acherra Asher yelled with urgency.

The Hollowkin-Janny pursued, limbs contorting unnaturally, its voice a discordant symphony of screams, as if three mouths shrieked in unison.

Simone careened around the corner just as they hurtled into the side yard. "Oh my GOD, is that Mr. Thacker?!" she shrieked, eyes wide with horror.

"Was Mr. Thacker," Theo corrected grimly, skidding into view, wielding a flashlight like a desperate sword.

Janny howled with demonic glee and leapt, limbs flailing wildly, a trash bin sent flying, briefly morphing into a flaming skull before stabilizing.

"I hate this town!" Simone screamed, her voice cutting through the chaos as she took off again, Theo just a step behind.

The Ashers veered left, luring Janny down the alley. Surface Asher spun and hurled a blazing bolt of light, scorching the Hollowkin just enough to halt its frenzied advance.

"Up the fire escape!" Acherra Asher commanded.

They scrambled up the ancient, groaning metal stairs as Janny slammed into the base, sending violent tremors through the entire structure.

From the rooftop, they gasped for air, gazing upon the town's nightmarish spectacle. Streets tore open. Time twisted violently sideways.

And far below, Janny's maniacal laughter echoed, fading as it vanished into the next flickering ruin.

———————————————————————

The following morning, a fragile new day unfolded in the kitchen where Lizzie stood, her gaze fixed upon her mother with an unsettled mix of wonder and trepidation. Something imperceptibly different filled the space.

Christine Marlowe moved through the room with an unnaturally smooth rhythm, her every motion a precise, practiced ballet as she flipped pancakes, brewed rich, aromatic coffee, and hummed a faded lullaby that Lizzie couldn't quite place from her childhood. Yet there was an unsettling quality to her graceful movements—her actions were too fluid, her eyes too distant, as if she were partially adrift in another realm.

"Mom?" Lizzie ventured hesitantly.

Her mother looked up, her smile broad but empty, as if it merely scratched the surface of a deeper, unspoken melancholy. "Morning, sweetheart. Hungry?"

"Kind of," Lizzie replied, pausing uncertainly. "Can I ask you something... peculiar?"

Christine chuckled softly, setting a warm plate on the counter with a deliberate clink of porcelain. "When has that ever stopped you?"

"Do you... remember anything about a tunnel?"

For but a split second, her mother's expression faltered— an imperceptible flicker of recognition dancing behind her eyes. "A tunnel?" she repeated, her tone tentative. "You mean the hiking trail behind the drive-in?"

"No," Lizzie pressed, stepping closer, her words laced with urgency. "A glowing tunnel. One that resonates with an almost musical hum. It's etched with symbols, mysterious and ancient. You saw it, didn't you?"

"Are you okay, honey? That sounds an awful lot..." Christine paused as if a she was trying to piece a puzzle together in her mind.

"...like a dream," Lizzie coaxed her mother gently.

"Exactly like a dream, I..." her mom trailed off once more. Lizzie could see the war within her mother's mind, subconscious battling with a lost memory.

"The tunnel that changes, mom," Lizzie said, taking her mom by the hand. "At the end of that tunnel..."

Christine blinked slowly, her hands trembling ever so slightly as they reached for a fragile ceramic mug. "I... dreamt about it," she whispered, her voice barely carrying above the hum of the morning. "Long ago, I thought it was merely a cruel dream. But sometimes, I still see it—the sensation of falling, and a voice calling out to me. It spoke my name... though not truly my name."

Lizzie felt her breath hitch, the notion hanging thickly in the air. "Mom... I think you've merged," she murmured, the revelation both terrifying and tender.

Christine lifted her eyes, now glassy and reflective, "What does that mean?"

"It means part of you isn't from here," Lizzie explained softly. "You've lived two lives at once—one in this world, and another in Acherra."

Acherra, the pretend place from her dreams. Her invisible friend used to live in that place. A shadow of wistfulness crossed her mother's face as she murmured, "I remember a city made entirely of shimmering stars, and voices that echoed around me—my voice, yet not entirely mine. I hid it away, afraid I was losing myself."

"You're not lost," Lizzie assured her, her voice filled with determined compassion. "You are among the first—a bridge between two realms."

Christine suddenly took measure of her daughter, the pieces falling into alignment, no longer fragmented. It all made sense again. That was the moment horror hit her. It wasn't supposed to make sense again, they had made sure of it. That was the pact. "Lizzie, how do you know of Acherra and the merged?"

Slowly, Lizzie recounted everything that had happened over the last two weeks all the way up to that moment. "Mom, we have to stop the ascension or everyone will merge and then it's game over! Meridra says we can, she's the one that told me about you. She told me you were able to control your merge and that it was successful."

Sinking slowly into a chair, her mother absorbed the weight of her dual existence. "Then why does everything around me feel like it's falling apart?"

Because it was.

That afternoon, Southridge didn't just tremble—it glitched in a surreal dance of chaos and confusion. Reality itself hiccuped in erratic fits and starts, as though a cosmic hand had shaken the world like a snow globe. A massive sinkhole yawned open in the high school parking lot, its gaping maw like an angry mouth ready to swallow everything in its path. It devoured asphalt and an entire row of junior parking spots, leaving nothing but a jagged chasm behind. Nearby, another rift tore through the old gas station, greedily consuming the pumps and a neatly stacked pyramid of windshield wiper fluid with a single gulp.

The town stuttered and shivered in a bizarre rhythm. An ice cream shop blinked into a shattered ruin, debris scattered like confetti, only to snap back into its cheerful pink existence as if nothing had happened. Streetlights flickered in reverse, casting eerie shadows that stretched unnaturally toward the midday sun. The air was charged with a faint taste of electricity, reminiscent of the tense moment just before a lightning strike.

Time wasn't broken, but it was definitely drunk, staggering through the moments with a tipsy unpredictability. Theo stepped off the curb, mid-text, when an unexpected chill gripped him. It wasn't the kind of chill born from wind or shade, but a bone-deep whisper that urged, "Run."

Across the street, a figure emerged from the distortion. It had the same shaggy curls, the same worn hoodie, and an incredulous expression that mirrored his own.

It was him—or at least, a version of him.

Theo stared, eyes wide with disbelief. So did the double. Then, in a bizarre twist, his doppelgänger raised a hand and waved, as if this were the most natural encounter in the world.

Theo blinked, struggling to comprehend. "Are... are you me?"

The double tilted its head, mirroring his confusion, mouthing, "Are you me?" It then shrugged nonchalantly, stuffed both hands in its pockets, and started walking toward Theo... but in a surreal moonwalk.

"What the —" Theo breathed, bewildered.

"Nice hoodie," Doppel-Theo muttered as he passed, his tone somehow both sarcastic and offended. "Bit tight in the shoulders though."

"Excuse me?" Theo spun around, utterly flabbergasted. "This hoodie is vintage! I got it at a flea market in—hey! Are you glitching my metabolism too?!"

The double paused mid-step, eyes wide with exaggerated horror. "Wait... do we share stomachs? Oh god. That burrito earlier was a mistake."

Before Theo could respond, the double smirked, offered a lazy salute, and vanished into thin air with a soft pop, leaving behind only the faint smell of static and... taco sauce?

Theo stood dumbfounded, heart pounding in his chest, staring at the empty sidewalk where his other-self had just been moments ago. The world around him felt surreal, like a dream teetering on the edge of reality.

Behind him, an ice cream truck rolled by, its warped sing-song warning echoing weirdly through the neighborhood. At the wheel, a red-eyed, purple-skinned Hollowkin waved and cackled maniacally as it passed.

Theo didn't stop running until he burst through Lizzie's front door, breathless and wide-eyed, the strange encounter replaying in his mind like a bizarre fever dream.

Just as the two Ashers were settling into the uneasy quiet of the living room—with their eyes occasionally flickering to the shifting shadows on the walls and fingers curling around glasses of water, ceremoniously passed to them by Mrs. Quinn, who insisted on dubbing it "emotion juice"—the overhead lights began to behave strangely. They shivered with a single flicker, then another, until finally bursting into a radiant flash of silver-blue that bathed the room in an otherworldly glow. A low, mechanical hum vibrated through the air, accompanied by the surreal sight of the mirror hanging in the hallway closet. It began to ripple like the surface of a disturbed pond, as if something beneath it sought to emerge.

In that charged moment, Mr. Quinn paused mid-slice of toast, his knife hovering over its intended target. "Unscheduled energy signature detected," he announced with a steady, measured tone that belied the tension.

At the same time, Mrs. Quinn caught her breath, her spatula grasped tightly mid-air as if suspended in time. "Possible breach in existential perimeter," she intoned, her voice a mix of urgency and routine, "engaging guest welcome subroutine—armed hug mode deactivated," a phrase that seemed to blend technical jargon with an oddly familiar domestic charm.

Then, with a shimmer of otherworldly light, the mirror surged outward like a living, liquid sheet. From within its undulating depths stepped Meridra—regal in every aspect. Her presence was commanding, her cloak billowing dramatically behind her, trailing eddies of stardust across the polished linoleum floor like reels of forgotten celestial secrets.

Meridra surveyed the two Ashers with a bittersweet smile, the sadness in her eyes deepened by ancient wisdom. "I've found you. But we don't have time," she declared in a voice that resonated with both authority and gentle sorrow.

The Ashers—taken aback by her sudden arrival—stammered in unison, "Meridra—?"

Her expression somber, the lines of concern etching her face, she responded without delay, "Gather them. All of them. We meet now."

Surface Asher glanced around the room in bewilderment, his eyes drifting to the oddly contoured couch. "Like... here? Because the couch is weird."

"No," Meridra replied firmly, the gravity of her words slicing through the tension. "Below. Where it's safe. Before the town unravels any further."

Mr. Quinn, regaining his composure, straightened his back as if preparing for battle. "Is this a merge party?" he inquired, his tone a mix of humor and unease.

Meridra's eyes hardened as she responded, "No. This is a war council."

Within the hour, the air around the Quinn home shifted dramatically. Lizzie, Theo, and Simone were ushered through a corridor now glowing with an eerie, pulsating light, leading them into a subterranean chamber beneath Quarry Lane. The chamber pulsed with life; ancient scrolls floated serenely above their heads, casting ghostly shadows, while bioluminescent roots wound through the walls like vibrant, living veins carrying the luminescence of distant stars.

Standing before them all, Meridra's cloak settled gracefully as the intense silver light dimmed into a softer gleam. Her voice, quiet yet resonant, broke the silence. "The Ascension," she murmured, "is no longer theory. It is no longer prophecy. It is now. You've seen the signs: the shifting buildings, the multiplying Hollowkin, the people losing themselves to chaos."

Theo, his face etched with grim determination, nodded as he recalled his bizarre encounter. "And, uh, I chased myself down Main Street, so yeah, that was new."

Meridra's gaze swept slowly over each weary soul, her words laden with urgency. "You have days. Maybe less. The fracture between your world and Acherra is stretching thin. The Architect aims to force the Merge across all humanity—and he's nearly ready."

A heavy hush fell over the gathered group. Lizzie exchanged a determined look with Asher—both of them caught in the mutual understanding of impending peril—and then turned to address her friends with resolute clarity.

"Then we find the Broken Citadel," she declared, her voice cutting through the silence like a clarion call, "and we stop him."

Simone cracked her knuckles, the sound echoing in the vast chamber. "Do we get swords this time?" she asked, half in jest, half in readiness.

Lizzie's eyes shone with an unwavering conviction. "We get answers," she said, her tone promising that truth, no matter how painful, was the only weapon worth brandishing.

"And maybe swords," Theo muttered hopefully, a small smile briefly flickering across his face.

At that moment, the chamber pulsed once again, a rhythmic beat that seemed to synchronize with the racing of their hearts. Outside, the ground trembled, its pulses a harbinger of the chaos to come.

And far away, beneath the fragile veil separating their world from another, something ancient and immense stirred—a secret force rising from the depths of both realms.

Chapter 15: The Architect

The night in Southridge shattered like a brittle mirror—splintering reality into shards that scattered across rooftops, alleys, and backyards. Although the stars still shimmered overhead, their placements felt fundamentally askew, as if they—a chorus of hesitant spectators—moved with uncertain, nervous glints whenever they thought they were unobserved.

A feathery fog slithered along the sidewalks, wrapping itself around gutters and seeping through hedges with an almost tender reluctance. It carried the texture of a hesitant breath—warm yet softly whispering secrets of disquiet. Even the insects seemed to fall mute in the midst of such an ambiQuinnnt night. The streetlights emitted a low hum, casting light that seemed more half-hearted than illuminating. Night did not feel entirely like night—it was suspended in a state of unsettling indecision.

In the cramped refuge beneath Quarry Lane, the group simmered with an inner unrest. Lizzie sat cross-legged on the cold stone floor, her fingers tracing the worn edges of her glyph shard—a shard that now pulsed with a warming intensity, like an echo of a long-buried heartbeat stirring conflict within her. Simone half-slept on a pile of rumpled sleeping bags, one shoe abandoned, the other clutching a flashlight as if it might banish the swirling doubts. Theo, huddled against a somber wall, feverishly scribbled equations into a notebook under the wavering glow of a drifting glyph-scroll, each equation mirroring his inner turmoil. And Asher—Surface Asher—rested on a lone cot in the shadowy corner, his body motionless while his mind roiled with questions and reluctance.

The Dream

It descended as subtly as the pause between lightning and thunder. One moment Asher lay beneath a pale stone ceiling, and in the next pulse of disbelief, he found himself standing on an endless plane of smooth black glass. There was no sky, no steady stars—only infinite, conflicted reflections of himself. Asher saw versions of himself: tall and short, aged and youthful, fragmented and whole. Some of these reflections wept in regret, others screamed in defiance, and one quietly knelt, bearing a smile that spoke of both terror and calm acceptance.

And then, slicing through the layered silence, came the voice.

"You are afraid."

It was a voice without volume—a presence that filled every crevice of his hearing, every bone, every shadow behind his eyes. It spoke not in a rush but in the steady cadence of inevitability.

"You do not know which version of yourself is truly real. That very uncertainty breeds your hesitation."

Asher spun in the shifting mirage.

Before him stood a figure—a man, if such a term could capture the enigma before him.

He embodied a contradiction, being both everything and nothing at once. His face morphed through infinite combinations: youthful yet ancient, at once unmistakably familiar yet strangely alien. His eyes, shifting through every hue imaginable, swirled like fractured prisms in a storm of conflict. Clad in robes woven from impossible geometry that defied rational perception, he did not walk; he simply existed—drawing closer with a presence heavy with unspoken tension.

"I was once like you," the Architect murmured, his tone soft yet laden with a bitter, unresolved conflict. "Divided. Torn. Dragged in too many directions at once."

The void pulsed, echoing with his conflicted past.

"But I chose unity."

Asher's throat felt parched with disbelief. "You... merged?"

"I did. I found every discarded, splintered version of myself and, despite the inner battles, I welcomed them in."

The Architect lifted his hand, and the obsidian surface beneath Asher's feet fractured into hundreds of shards. In each splinter, Asher witnessed another version of himself: one reaching out to clasp Lizzie's hand in hesitant solidarity, one standing over a field of Hollowkin corpses with a mixture of sorrow and resolve, one with glyphs scorched into his skin, laughing in a manner both divine and conflicted.

"You pursue the illusion of identity," the Architect intoned, his head tilting as myriad conflicting expressions played across his ever-changing features. "But identity is tenuous—in its fragmentation, you are doomed to endless dissent. It is better to be whole. Immortal. Untouchable."

"You've lost yourself entirely," Asher whispered, his voice quivering with the weight of his inner discord.

The Architect's smile morphed, reflecting every guise he had ever worn.

"Asher... neither do you."

Southridge—The Real World

Asher awoke with a choked gasp, his lungs seizing with a desperate urgency akin to the final exhalation of a drowning man reaching for air. His hair clung to his scalp in damp strands, the sweat soaking the edges of his pillow a tangible testament to the nightmares that had plagued him. His heart pounded relentlessly, each beat an accusatory rhythm echoing against his ribs, as if it were aligned with the haunting dream rather than his waking self.

The glyphs tattooed on his arms glowed faintly in the dim light, a soft luminescence that seemed to pulse with the memory of the dream, like a spectral reflection from another realm. Instantly, Lizzie was by his side, her eyes a mix of anxiety and fierce determination as they searched his face for answers.

"Are you okay?" she asked, her voice a careful balance of fear and comfort, like the gentle lull of a mother soothing a child. Her hand reached out, warm and steady, anchoring him against the shivering uncertainty of the waking world. Asher shook his head, the motion firm and resolute, not the least bit defeated.

"He's real," he declared, his voice heavy with the burden of revelation, the words echoing softly in the underground chamber where they sat. Lizzie's brow furrowed, her expression a complex interplay of worry and acknowledgment, understanding the significance of his words before he even spoke them.

"Who?" she inquired, though her question was more a confirmation of shared knowledge than a demand for explanation. She understood the gravity of his vision, even before he uttered the name.

"The Architect," Asher replied, his words thick with both conviction and terror. The name lingered in the air, suspending time and motion, casting a shadow over the room as they both absorbed the implications of his revelation.

Elsewhere in Town

Outside, the Hollowkin began to stir.

From storm drains and alley shadows, from cracks between worn and fragile sidewalk stones, they slithered and crawled into the moonlit streets. Their numbers multiplied with each passing second, a grotesque army of grotesque tens and hundreds—then more.

The Hollowkin's glistening forms rippled in sinister harmony with the uneven light, some taking on the unsettling shapes of faceless children while others twisted into fractured, walking mirrors. Their eyes gleamed with an eerie, lifeless hunger that cast a chilling glow upon the darkened world around them. And trailing ominously behind them, released from the forgotten ruins below, was something far worse than them all: a massive, four-legged Hollowkin construct—a monstrous, nightmarish fusion of twisted limbs and half-merged souls, with the body of an unholy beast.

It howled at the empty, uncaring sky like a machine choking on prayer, then galloped down Main Street with terrifying speed, the sound of its steps a deafening harbinger of dread.

A group of teens near the Waffle Shack vanished with a blink. Their phones hit the sidewalk still ringing, still displaying unanswered calls for help that never came. The Hollowkin swarmed through the town, a living wave of chaos and panic.

Simone awoke with a start. "What was that noise?"

Theo held up his scroll. "Um. Guys? We're not alone out there."

Visions

As night deepened around them, Lizzie began to perceive it—not clearly, not like seeing something solid and certain—but in scattered flashes, moments that abruptly pierced her thoughts and wove the tangible world with threads of uncertainty. Her vision blurred between possibilities, teetering between the real and the unreal, between the present and the looming future.

Acherra seeped into Southridge, like ink slowly spreading across a page, dissolving boundaries that once seemed unchangeable. She saw the trees from her world intertwining wildly with telephone poles, nature carelessly unfurling, indifferent to human-made structures. She saw ancient ruins hovering like cursed specters above the water tower, their ghostly stillness contradicting their chaotic intrusion.

Time itself shattered like waves breaking, folding back upon themselves—classroom bells ringing in reverse, her father's image flickering between laughter and silence, warmth and absence, caught in the span of a single breath. In one flicker, the town was a peaceful suburb—a familiar refuge under a serene starlit sky.

In the next, it was a ruin—illuminated by crystal veins pulsing with alien light, haunted by fractal shadows and silver winds that howled with an eerie chill, echoing through the shattered remains of everything she knew. Lizzie stumbled, the visions crashing into her like a prophecy fulfilled. Her eyes widened, filled with a tumultuous mix of shock and reluctant acceptance. She blinked hard, once, twice, shaking her head as if to dispel the haunting glimpses, yet she was torn by a resolute certainty that this was the truth, that this was the Ascension, and it was upon them.

It was now.

The Dream Asher described—his warning—seemed less fantastical with each passing second. She turned to the others, her heart pounding with a mix of urgency and doubt, understanding and confusion. She had to make them see, to grasp the full weight of their situation, to comprehend before it was too late, yet she herself wavered on the brink of disbelief.

The Decision

Back underground, the moments ticked with a heartbeat urgency. Meridra stepped through the veil of worlds, her breath a shadow and her eyes heavy with knowing. She stood still, just for a second, surveying their strain, their inward spiral. She locked her gaze onto Asher.

"He touched your dream, didn't he?" she said softly, each word a thread of consequence.

Asher sat up, almost shivering with the recollection. "He offered… peace. Wholeness." His voice wavered between intrigue and dread, his mind still a prisoner of the Architect's fractured promise.

Simone stood with her flashlight, her sleep-heavy eyes sparking with curiosity and sarcasm. "So, the guy's like, what? Some creepy multiversal therapist?"

"No," Meridra said, as certain as stone. "He was the first. The first Merge." She paused, letting the weight of her words settle into the fissures of their fear. "And now, he's trying to bring everything down with him."

Lizzie reached into her pocket, her resolve burning hotter than the fear. She gripped the shard until her knuckles ached, until pain and determination were indistinguishable. "We don't let him," she said, her voice a steely bandage against the hurt and horror.

Meridra looked to the distance as if seeing past walls and worlds—seeing toward the deepest part of Acherra, where the battle for their futures had already begun. "Then we must go to the Hollow's Core. Where the Architect prepares the final glyphwork." Her words gathered in their ears like a storm, adrenaline rushing in their veins like wind.

"Let me guess," Theo said, already gathering his bag with a weary grin. "We're gonna need snacks."

Lizzie smirked, a crack of levity in the gravity pulling them down. "And probably weapons."

Simone knelt, tying her shoelaces. She fastened them as if they were armor, as if they might carry her through more than the chasms of two broken worlds. The flashlight in her hand flickered, casting long shadows against the wall, each shadow a ghost of their struggle.

"It's collapsing faster than we planned," Asher said, a grim understanding gnawing at his resolve. "We need to hurry."

A tense silence wrapped around them, binding them to the moment, forcing them to feel the breathlessness of now. In that silence, they heard it: the distant rush of Hollowkin swarming across the fracture.

"Yeah, that means running" said Theo, his eyes wide with nothing to hide behind. "always running."

Outside, the sky cracked silently overhead, and from the flickering edge of the street, something ancient began to walk.

Chapter 16: The Glyphwake

They returned to Acherra like lightning striking twice—fast, sharp, and undeniably charged. The air ripped apart with their haste, a vivid crack between worlds that marked their arrival with visceral urgency. The slanted tunnel behind the Crestline Drive-In groaned as it opened again, each creak a protest that echoed their need for speed, the rippling threshold breathing them back into the pulsing dream-realm. Only this time, the world beyond the veil had changed. Acherra's colors were sharper, more fevered, a landscape drenched in hues of madness and panic. The air tasted like ozone and memory, and every breath felt like it had been lived before. A sourceless hum of impending collapse filled the space between heartbeats.

"We're running out of time," Lizzie muttered as her boots struck the glowing earth, urgency lacing her voice like wildfire. The glyph shard in her hand was burning hot, a molten core searing her palm. It was as if the world around them throbbed in response to their presence, aware of their mission and the stakes they carried.

Ahead, Meridra was waiting. She stood poised, a figure of calm amidst the chaos, as if she had always belonged to this altered place. "The Glyphwake calls," she said, nodding toward a distant, luminous canyon where the ground shimmered like melted glass, incandescence rising from it like heatwaves. Her words sparked a new urgency, a reminder of purpose. "But not all of you can go."

Theo glanced sideways, anticipation and dread warring in his eyes. He already sensed the plan, the inevitable strategy. "Let me guess... we're splitting the party."

"You and Simone will stay above," Meridra instructed, her voice cutting through the charged air with determined precision. "There are counter-glyphs—old failsafes buried in your world. They must be activated in tandem with the glyph anchors in the Glyphwake." Her gaze held steady, a silent will for them to succeed against impossible odds.

Simone groaned. "Why do I feel like this is going to involve a lot of running and near-death experiences?" Her sarcasm barely masked the fear beneath. Yet, a flicker of resolve danced in her stance, a readiness for the challenge.

"It always does," Theo said with a half-smile, adjusting his backpack with an air of resigned adventure. He pulled out the laminated glyph map they'd copied from Meridra's archive, the lines and runes glowing like a premonition. "Let's get mystical."

The two of them vanished into a warp-gate toward the surface—Theo muttering something about needing a proper breakfast before activating ancient magical artifacts. Their departure left a fleeting echo, a constricting pressure that vanished as quickly as it came.

Lizzie turned to the two Ashers, her eyes burning with determination. This was their moment, their split-second chance to change their fate. "Let's find the Glyphwake."

The Descent

The journey down was like falling through a kaleidoscope of time and stone, a dizzying descent into the very marrow of existence. Lizzie, Surface Asher, and Acherra Asher followed a spiraling stair carved deep into the bones of the world—each ancient step lined with glyphs that seemed to awaken, pulsing with spectral light in response to their presence. The deeper they went, the warmer the air grew until it wrapped around them like a living thing, a sweltering reminder of how far they had come, how near the urgency of their mission lay. Memories rose around them, towering walls alive with flickering echoes that whispered and sang, a cacophony of all the lives that had tried and failed before.

They stepped into the Glyphwake.

It was a canyon turned inside out, an impossible expanse of history and ruin—thousands of floating tablets, orbs, and crystalline veins suspended midair in concentric rings, like a shattered halo orbiting a dark, churning core. Each artifact spun with a delicate violence, etched with glyphs: names, memories, laws. The ancestral record of every Merge attempt in history. A city of broken dreams and forgotten hopes.

"It's beautiful," Surface Asher whispered, his voice a reverent hush over the riot of forms.

Acherra Asher's eyes narrowed, tracing the furious throb of the central core. "And terrifying," he added, a shiver of fear creeping into his voice. "That's where it stores the failures."

As if summoned by his words, the canyon shifted. A shimmer of light erupted from the nearest wall of crystal and projected a memory into the space around them, wrapping them in its eerie glow.

A town—eerily similar to Southridge—burned in violet flame. Buildings crumbled into voids. People screamed as their reflections turned against them. Two boys tried to Merge. They didn't finish. The explosion wiped out everything.

"Lysfield, 1912," Meridra's voice echoed faintly from the glyphwork, her words ghostly and unyielding. "One of the first Ascensions attempted too early. The Merge wasn't clean. The town blinked off the map. Your newspapers called it a mine collapse."

Lizzie stepped closer to the memory, her heart pounding a frantic beat against ribcage and fear. Her eyes filled with horror and resolve as the fragmented visions tore against the fragile certainty she clung to, the certainty that they could stop this, that they could succeed where so many had failed.

Another flare lit the canyon.

A cathedral in the desert, 1965. Another Ascension. The glyph anchor cracked. The people vanished, their voices trapped in the stone like insects in amber. An entire city swallowed by silence and time, never to be found again.

"This is what we're stopping," Lizzie breathed, her voice barely more than a whisper as she steeled herself against the awful truth.

The canyon erupted with new light, a splintering burst of merciless memories.

A university town, 1979. Buildings grew and shattered as time distorted its own passage. People staggered in horror as their bodies twisted into impossible shapes, as their lives stretched and collapsed into nothingness.

An island town, 1888. A lighthouse burned like a beacon of despair as it was overtaken by spectral shades and the last shadows of its inhabitants. A mother's scream pierced the air, her child's shadow grinning back at her.

A city on the coast, 1944. The glyph anchors glowed, then dimmed, then glowed again. Sirens wailed as the streets flooded with water and Hollowkin, drowning the world in an unstoppable tide.

Lizzie faltered under the weight of it all, grief and determination clashing within her like storm, like fire.

Fractured light poured over them in dizzying waves, each new memory a punch to the gut, a fresh horror to digest and discard. They pushed deeper into the Glyphwake, their intent unbroken despite the Lizzielanche of failure that pummeled them from all sides, the generations of pain and ruin that wrapped around them like a brutal mantle.

A pedestal hovered at the heart of the canyon, a jagged altar gleaming with impossible brightness. The three reached it, breathless and determined, where they found the anchor glyphs for both worlds intricately joined.

The Revelation

At the center of the Glyphwake stood a pedestal, a jagged altar gleaming with impossible brightness. Two anchor glyphs—one for surface, one for Acherra—intertwined like vines of mirrored stone, hovered at its core. From a distance, it looked like a relic of crystal and bone, a fragile thing made monstrous by its potential to destroy.

"They're incomplete," Acherra Asher said, his voice part wonder, part fear. He took in every detail, every line and curve that meant hope, that meant despair. "They need something."

"They need us," Lizzie replied, her breath quickening, her mind racing to every memory that had burned its way into the Glyphwake, every horror that had claimed lives and futures. Her hand found his and held on tightly, as if their contact were the only bridge that might span certainty and collapse.

As her shard touched the glyph anchor, it flared gold, blinding and urgent. Acherra Asher stepped forward, and the twin flare met hers—silver spiraling through the air like thread, like possibility.

The glyph anchors responded—clicking into motion like an ancient engine waking from slumber, an apparatus of ruin and salvation powering to life.

A projection burst into the air like a violent dream. They saw it all: two versions of themselves. One half-merged. One broken apart. One... fused.

"The law can be rewritten," Meridra's voice echoed again from the relentless history. "If the bridge is strong enough."

Lizzie and Asher looked at each other, their eyes raw with hope and terror. They saw through each other—through the years and the worlds, through every failed attempt. Not just as friends. As halves of something ancient, woven through time and possibility.

"If we Merge here, just enough to rewrite the glyph code…" Lizzie said, her voice shaking with the enormity of their plan, the urgency of their gamble.

"We can sever the tether," Acherra Asher finished, his words a lifeline, an anchor against doubt. "Acherra won't fold into the surface."

"For now," Surface Asher added, a thread of fear lacing his resolve. "But the Architect will come."

They turned to the glyph anchors, possibility spiraling around them, stakes higher than hope.

And placed their hands down.

Meanwhile, on the Surface

Theo and Simone sprinted headlong through the shifting chaos that was Southridge Cemetery. The ground beneath them writhed with uncertainty, one moment solid and the next an insubstantial shimmer of flickering gravestones. They ducked and wove, outpacing shadows that loomed and dissolved, breathing in frantic gulps as they ran. Time itself was an erratic hunter, shifting around them in merciless pursuit; at one breath, it was day—a harsh, unforgiving sun baking the earth—and at the next, evening clutched the world with its spectral fingers, the moon cutting through gathering clouds that hadn't existed moments before.

"Remind me again how activating an ancient glyph behind the gym turned into being chased by a skeleton with my aunt's face?!" Simone yelled, her voice half panic, half begrudging thrill.

"Merge echoes!" Theo gasped between breaths, his mind racing to stay ahead of the chaos unfolding around them. His footfalls crunched against the blurring transition from grass to gravel, each step a leap into the unknown. "Very cranky!"

The scenery warped, shifted, and they were at the center of the burial ground, closing in on their target—the second counter-glyph beneath the cemetery's oldest statue.

Theo skidded to a halt, fumbling in his pack for the second shard. It leapt into his hand before he could grab it, pulsing like a heartbeat eager for life. Without skipping a beat, he jammed it onto the glyph stone.

The ground shuddered as if in reply. Lines of blue fire erupted from the point of contact, crawling across the grass like veins, like the very earth had come alive to witness their mission.

Simone grinned, the adrenaline of success and the nearness of danger fueling her resolve. "That's two. One more."

"Drive-in next," Theo huffed, already in motion, already feeling the rush of worlds collapsing behind him.

"I'm never eating popcorn again," Simone muttered as they raced into the unknown, the thrill of pursuit and the promise of escape hot on their heels.

Back in Acherra

As the glyph anchors flared with urgency and light, as they vibrated with need and danger, Lizzie felt the weight of her very soul stretch and tremble within her. She gasped as a vision overtook her: Southridge coated in Acherra's glow, the two worlds folding into one as they had in so many past attempts.

Trees made of crystal growing beside Walmart.

Hollowkin chasing school buses.

Time rupturing in sudden, overlapping loops that trapped entire lives in inescapable circles. A hundred versions of catastrophe, each more devastating than the last. She saw everyone she knew, everyone she loved, caught in its orbit. And she saw herself standing at the center of it all—part Lizzie, part something more. A bridge. A new possibility.

Asher gripped her hand tighter. "Just a little longer," he urged, his voice a lifeline pulling her back from despair.

The Glyphwake pulsed—deep and low, like the heartbeat of the world. It vibrated around them, a shuddering testament to their refusal to fail, to their reckless hope.

They held on, the tether unbroken, unrelenting. But it had been rewritten.

In the deepest ruin of Acherra, the Architect turned his head. He felt the shift. And he began to move.

Chapter 17: The Hollow Crown

Reality cracked at the edges, bending and shattering like a brittle thing torn apart by its own design. Not metaphorically. Not subtly. Southridge trembled with visible seams, glitching and warping like a half-rendered simulation, a reality unspooling at the seams.

Fragments of existence flickered like disobedient ghosts.

Entire houses blinked in and out of being, one instant imposing structures, the next empty voids that swallowed space and time.

A dog chased itself in infinite loops, its howl echoing in endless cycles before becoming the bark of something else.

A stop sign screamed before melting into a tree, its limbs gnarled, its leaves tangled and artificial.

The Hollowkin had changed.

What once crawled and skittered now walked with fluid confidence, bold and adaptive. Some even smiled, their faces disturbingly human.

Theo had just watched a man wave at his own reflection before dissolving into a puddle of light—and then reforming as someone else entirely. "That was Coach Berman," Theo whispered, horrified. The words came out as if they might burst apart in his mouth, full of disbelief and fear. "He just—he became Mrs. Donahue."

Beside him, Simone was furiously scratching at a piece of sidewalk with a glyph-tipped pen, trying to stabilize the ground beneath them, trying to stop the chaos from getting worse. "Yeah, well, tell Mrs. Donahue she owes me five bucks and a new reality."

Across town, the high school had become a battlefield of flickering dimensions, a war zone of shifting scenes. Lockers hissed, students merged and unmerged in bursts of static. A Hollowkin masquerading as the janitor had taken over the PA system to scream ancient poetry in reverse Latin. Shadows filled the halls, and debris hovered as if caught between gravity and flight.

Lizzie stood frozen in the midst of it all, the glyph shard pulsing violently in her hand, her heart beating in frantic tandem. Behind her, the town shimmered—and before her stood herself.

Only not herself.

The other Lizzie stepped out from a ripple in the world, an echo with substance, a possibility with breath. Her hair shimmered like glass-thread, eyes flickering with symbols, an alien thing cloaked in familiarity. Her voice was layered—hers and not hers, a chorus of one. "You're late."

Lizzie stumbled backward, gripping her shard like a weapon. "You're me."

"I'm what you become if you complete the Merge," the doppelgänger said with a twisted smile that was both Lizzie's and not. "Or if you don't. We're branching."

"Is that a threat?" The words left Lizzie's mouth in a rush she couldn't control.

"No. It's a warning. If you resist the Merge, both worlds crack like mirrors dropped from too high a shelf. You'll watch everyone fracture from the inside out." Before Lizzie could respond, the world exploded.

Acherra burst into view like an overlaid image, the sky rippling as Hollowkin poured through the seams. They weren't hiding anymore. They didn't need to. Their forms flickered between shadow and flesh, some with too many eyes, others with none. A four-limbed creature emerged from behind a Southridge grocery store and folded itself into a teenager.

No one blinked.

The war had begun.

In Acherra

Asher—both of them—stood in the fractured forest just beyond the Glyphwake. The trees bled light, and the ground pulsed beneath them like a dying star, a brilliant, fading heartbeat trembling as it threatened to tear apart. From the misted woods around them, from a haze that blurred vision and reality and certainty, emerged something new. They froze as it came into focus; something they had never seen; something they had never dared to imagine.

A Hollowkin.

But different.

Its form was humanoid, and it still had the purplish hue to its skin but its red eyes glowing softly—not with hunger, but grief. "I surrender," it said in perfect English, hands raised in a gesture that seemed almost human, almost familiar, almost too close.

The Ashers exchanged a look, the shock of its words, the horror of its shape, warring with their instincts to run or to fight or to collapse beneath the weight of this new possibility. Hope and terror wrestled on their faces.

"You what?" Surface Asher asked, disbelieving, his voice cracking as he spoke.

The creature knelt. It seemed to shudder, to flicker with the light trembling like a living thing around it. "I defect. I was human once. We all were. Before he took us."

"Who's he?" Acherra Asher's voice was urgent, raw.

The Hollowkin's mouth twisted into something like a grimace, something like pain, as if talking were a new experience. "He calls self the Architect. But once was man. Like you."

The revelation hit them like a blow. Lizzie's vision of Hollowkin chasing skies filled with Walmart and school buses. The world held captive by the Architect.

The creature's next words were like a condemned man issuing his own sentence. It did not raise its voice; it did not need to. "He tried to Merge with every self he ever had—every potential version."

"And it drove him mad," Surface Asher whispered, haunted and horrified, the words leaving his mouth like an incantation.

"It made him immortal," the Hollowkin said, each word soaked with bitterness and history. "He became a god by shattering the mirror until only one reflection remained—his own."

Movement flickered in the distance.

"But we thought you all wanted to take over, to feast on us, to grow stronger and conquer the world," Acherra Asher pointed out, her voice tinged with both skepticism and curiosity.

The Hollowkin's pleading eyes, however, painted a picture of a different reality. "We are not all the same," he explained, his voice a mix of desperation and hope. "We different, like humans. The Architect controls what he can, but some of us have been yearning for freedom. Not all are bad. Some, though, very, very bad."

The Ashers exchanged glances, a silent understanding passing between them like an unspoken pact.

"What's your name?" Surface Asher inquired gently, her tone softening with compassion.

The question caught the Hollowkin off guard. His purplish skin shifted hues, deepening as though flushed with an unfamiliar emotion. "I was once called Ingy," he answered, a hint of nostalgia in his voice.

"Nice to meet you, Ingy," Acherra Asher said warmly, her smile wide and inviting as she extended a hand in friendship. "Welcome to the team."

Ingy's smile in return was genuine, his expression sincere and untainted by malice, a flicker of relief and gratitude lighting up his features.

They saw the Architect. They saw what he was becoming. They saw what he was. He pulled himself into existence, a specter with substance, a looming shadow forged from both absence and being. He was no longer a distant menace, no longer a hidden tormentor.

He was alive before them, a bridge between fear and inevitability. He was a walking contradiction of light and void, a paradox made flesh.

The Architect moved like a storm given form, each step a confident sweep of terror and certainty. The Hollow Crown sat upon his head, an unholy testament. He wore it like a king, like a curse, like a prophecy fulfilled.

They gazed in trembling awe and horror at what he had become. And he knew they were watching.

His presence loomed like an unwritten future, a terrifying promise that could not be broken. Glyphs refracted around him like shattered light, mirrored armor glistening with an impossible glow. His entire being rippled with power, with danger, with the histories of every self he had ever become. Hands like clockwork, a body of liquid steel, a face that shifted between identities so quickly it hurt to look. His shifting, terrifying face was all faces. The faces of a thousand fallen men. The faces of a thousand doomed gods.

He didn't speak. He didn't have to. His voice emerged in perfect stillness. His voice was every disappearance they had ever witnessed, every explosion they had ever failed to stop.

His words hit them like death. "I am the correction. The echo's end. The Merge is not your future. It is your inevitability."

Lizzie trembled as she watched, back in Acherra, back in Southridge, back in every world she had ever known. Her vision bled between realms, each one a kaleidoscope of fear. She felt it snap tighter. The tether. The future.

In her head she heard her doppel crying out, "we have to merge, Lizzie! Time has run out...for all of us."

It was happening.

Everything. Now.

Meridra and Christine appeared before her, grasping at Lizzie and pulling her in tight. They flashed out of existence and reappeared with the Ashers, pulling them in as well.

The world flickered like a dying bulb. Lizzie blinked, her heart racing as she tried to catch her breath. The shift was brutal, reality itself bending and snapping around them like the coils of a wounded beast.

They were in the Keepers' inner sanctum—a vast chamber pulsing with ancient light, its walls lined with shimmering glyphs that radiated an unearthly glow. Scrolls floated above them, lazy orbits transforming into frantic spins. They cast shadows that twisted like the fate of worlds, shadows that seemed alive with their own hungry urgency. A deep hum resonated through the space, a vibration that coursed through their bones and filled the air with an electric desperation.

Beside Lizzie stood Christine and Meridra, their faces taut with resolve and fear. Acherra Asher clutched Surface Asher's arm, both of their eyes wide with disbelief and awareness. Theo stumbled, catching himself on Simone's shoulder as he took in their sudden change of location. His mouth dropped open in shock.

"We just got warp-zapped!" he exclaimed, his voice thin with confusion and awe.

"This is it," Christine said gravely, her words lifting above the turmoil like a distant echo. "This is where we make our stand."

Lizzie barely recognized her mother; there was something almost spectral about her now—ethereal yet solid, as if she existed in two realms at once.

"They want us to Merge," Lizzie gasped, taking in the enormity of their situation. "We have to stop it."

Meridra nodded, her expression fierce and knowing. "We must disrupt the Architect's power before it collapses all into chaos."

Ingy emerged from the shadows—a silhouette at first, then clearer as he approached. His red eyes glowed not with malice but urgency.

"It's working," he rasped, his voice ragged yet hopeful as he gestured toward the glyphs that floated above them like stars thrown from their courses. "The others are breaking free."

Theo jumped back in terror. "Oh my god! It's a-a-a a thingy," he screamed, pointing wildly at the Hollowkin.

"Ingy," the Hollowkin corrected as it casually brushed by Theo as if it were the most normal thing in the world.

"He's with us," both Asher's said at the same time.

"Great," Theo retorted, "y'all are in stereo now!"

Simone looked skeptical but fierce. "I'm still armed," she declared, brandishing the flashlight like a weapon of old magic.

Surface Asher glanced at Meridra with wonder and suspicion intertwining in his gaze. "You're..."

"Here for you," she finished simply, offering him a smile heavy with history and love.

Lizzie's eyes burned with determination as she turned to each of them in turn—her friends, her family, her mirrors—and saw the same resolve mirrored back at her.

"Then let's do this," she said, her voice clear and hard as steel.

Ingy reached up to one of the glyph-scrolls above them; his touch sent it spiraling down in a cascade of light until it landed gently on Theo's outstretched hands.

"What is this?" Theo asked breathlessly, feeling its weightless importance settle into him.

"Blueprints," Ingy replied urgently. "The Architect's core— all his weakest points."

Theo scanned it quickly; unmistakable understanding flared across his face.

"It's a map!" he shouted triumphantly. "We can thread back through—the same way we came!"

"He won't let us get near him!" Surface Asher warned bitterly as memory flashed through him: fragments of an impossible dream where all futures died and still he lived.

Acherra Asher placed a hand on his shoulder— strengthened by the touch, emboldened by his own newfound resolve. "But we have to try."

Simone's eyes widened as she realized something: "The Glyphwake," she exclaimed. "That's where we split the tether!" Her voice leapt with an idea that fused desperation and hope.

Meridra nodded, gesturing to the Keepers' inner sanctum around them as if urging them to see it anew. "Exactly. We create an echo, a second loop of possibility," she explained. "One world surges ahead while the other slips behind. He cannot hold both!"

Christine placed a gentle hand on Lizzie's cheek, her touch light yet filled with reassurance. "You can do this, sweetheart," she said softly before casting a knowing glance at Meridra. "Do what we once couldn't."

"Create a rift within the rift," Meridra added with quiet insistence.

Realization dawned like wildfire across Lizzie's face—followed by trepidation and fierce determination. She took in the urgent faces around her, felt the world shudder beneath their feet, then turned toward the two Ashers who mirrored her every breath and heartbeat.

"We go back through," she said urgently, already moving toward the exit. Her eyes met Surface Asher's—a lifetime of shared destiny and untold futures passing between them in an instant.

The words left her lips strong and sure.

"Together."

Chapter 18: The Merge Field

They infiltrated the Architect's sanctum not with crude power but with intricate cunning. The Keepers' glyph-map served as their precise scalpel, slicing through the tangled folds of warped space and twisted dimension. Each glyph acted as a master stitch in a delicate tapestry, seamlessly threading them between collapsing layers of reality like secret smugglers navigating the endless corridors of time. This passageway was no ordinary door—it was a gaping rift, meticulously torn open by pulsing glyphs imbued with twin shards of energy and a fierce determination to defy annihilation.

Beyond the threshold lay the Merge Field. It was not a temple as convention demanded, but an ethereal space between spaces—a vast, suspended realm floating in a void awash with silver hues and ink-dark shadows. Here, fragments of every failed Ascension drifted in orbit like shattered constellations scattered across the heavens. Ghostly spires materialized and dissolved from the nothingness, forged out of raw memory and fundamental mistake, while living glyphs crawled through the air like sentient equations, continuously rewriting themselves with each ephemeral breath.

At the very heart of this surreal landscape stood the Anchor Nexus, a pulsating core of creation and fate. Flanking this cosmic beacon, with hands tightly clasped and eyes blazing with incandescent resolve, were Lizzie and the two incarnations of Asher. In that charged moment, the Merge began.

The entire field shuddered with energy as the glyphwork activated. Phantasmal echoes of alternate timelines flickered into life, dancing about like fireflies caught in an eternal summer night. Fragments of Southridge, echoes of Acherra, entire worlds fused and fissioned in a cascade of unimaginable possibilities—children mysteriously born of impossible crossings, and screams that reverberated backward through time.

Asher met the gaze of his other self—his mirror, his twin, his shadow. "This is it," he murmured, voice thick with determination. "We either become something whole, or we are torn apart by our own ambition."

A new voice, smooth and enigmatic as polished obsidian, cut through the tension. "Or," it intoned with otherworldly allure, "you could become something more."

In a sudden burst of refracted light, the Architect emerged—a prismatic entity clad in glimmering glyph-armor and liquid, ever-shifting shadow. He hovered above the field like a fallen star crowned in sublime darkness, the shimmering Hollow Crown resting regally upon his brow.

"You need not tear each other apart," he declared, his voice cascading through dimensions like rippling water. "Merge with me. Become the Key. Inherit the full spectrum of glyphs. Stabilize both realms and achieve eternal harmony."

At his words, the very field trembled as if trying to decide its own fate. Asher hesitated, feeling the irresistible pull of the Architect's offer surge through him like a promise wrought of pure, unyielding logic. A vivid vision unfurled in his mind—a unified world devoid of Hollowkin, free from pain and marked by seamless harmony. There was the tantalizing prospect of a singular, perfect self and purpose, with no room left for doubt.

Acherra Asher, too, felt the seductive clarity of perfection and peace calling him. But then Lizzie stepped forward, holding a blazing glyph shard in her palm that radiated a fierce, red heat. Her voice rang out, sharp and unwavering, cutting through the growing uncertainty.

"Asher," she warned, resolute and passionate, "he isn't offering us peace. He's offering submission. He does not seek to save these worlds—he wants to control them."

The Architect's eyes glinted with a cold, crystalline intensity. "I want to protect them," he insisted softly, almost tenderly.

"By turning everyone into replicas of you?" countered Lizzie, her tone slicing through the charged air. "By eliminating their flaws, their fears, and even their failures?"

Acherra Asher staggered, his mind clouded by the torrent of memories the field brutally unspooled, while Surface Asher clutched his head in a desperate bid to stave off the overwhelming pull of collapsing realities. Their thoughts flickered uncertainly, caught in a tumultuous tug-of-war between the lure of surrender and the fierce desire for resistance.

"Why are we even fighting this?" Surface Asher growled, a note of anger threading his voice. "Perhaps he's right. We are unstable by nature. One final Merge and we could become as fragmented as Lysfield. What if in doing so, we destroy everything and everyone we love?"

"Then we face failure head-on," Lizzie answered, slicing through the disarray as she stepped between them. Her entire being crackled with radiant light, while searing memories blazed beneath her skin. "We fight even harder. We burn even brighter. We seize back our choice."

The Architect then spread out his arms, and the shimmering glyphs across the field were drawn inward as if pulled by an unseen gravitational force. Bolts of lightning arced across the space, cleaving through the air as the very fabric around them twisted into razor-sharp threads capable of unmaking existence itself. "You choose death," he pronounced, his voice echoing ominously across the sprawling, precarious expanse.

Meanwhile...

Ingy, Simone, and Theo barreled through the outer corridor of the Merge Field, ducking under the chaos of collapsing timelines and vicious glyph storms shredding everything in their path. "This place is a waking nightmare, a labyrinth of cursed math problems!" Theo yelled, hurling a fractured energy disc that erupted in a blinding explosion, obliterating a swarm of insectoid echoes in its fiery wake.

"Keep moving!" Simone commanded, vaulting over a churning ripple in the floor that flickered violently between molten lLizzie and a bed of flowers. Her grip on the glyph-dagger was ironclad, a lifeline in the tempest.

Ingy halted abruptly, his red eyes flaring wide with urgency. "There!" he rasped, pointing to a seething seam of light at the chamber's edge. "The Architect's anchor— it's hemorrhaging instability into the Nexus."

Theo's eyes widened. "That's our opportunity?"

Ingy turned to face them, determination burning in his gaze. "If I can rend the glyph seam open, you'll have mere seconds to transmit the feedback loop—just enough to fracture his structure. But I'll be the one to hold it."

Simone's face contorted with a mix of fear and resolve. "What happens to you?"

Ingy offered a half-smile, both hollow and defiant. "I was born of the Hollowkin. I severed those ties. Let me be the one to destroy him completely."

With a primal roar, Ingy drove his claws into the seam, tearing reality itself apart. The light within was agony incarnate, screaming in a symphony of glyph-tone.

Theo thrust the shard into the feedback node with unwavering precision. Simone anchored himself to Theo's shoulders, bracing for the storm to come.

Amid the Roar of Acherra's Collapse

While Lizzie and the Ashers stood at the very center of the Merge Field, where twisting spirals of light dissolved into wild and indecipherable equations, the outskirts of Acherra—what little remained of it—plunged into a maelstrom of full-scale war. Chaos ruled without mercy. The very earth split apart beneath towering columns of ash and crystalline debris. What once were wooded groves now shimmered like fractured forests of glass, their branches shattering into huddles of spectral birds that shrieked as they were reborn from splinters. From the depths of fractured realities, the Hollowkin emerged; no longer relegated to the dark crevices of shadows, they now rampaged in plain sight—grotesque, shifting abominations whose forms warped in mid-stride with unsettling fluidity: legs transformed into wings while arms dissolved into writhing whips of flesh entwined with luminous energy. They spilled forth from tearing rifts like a swarm of insects fleeing a burning hive.

And yet, the Keepers fought back with fervent determination. Atop a jagged stone ridge overlooking the pandemonium, Meridra and Christine stood as steadfast bastions amid the clamor. Their cloaks whipped violently in the surging winds that carried the remnants of unraveling time, each gust a reminder of the fragility of their world. Below them, a surging tide of Hollowkin advanced, their shrieks a discordant symphony of warped hunger, their eyes aflame with glyphlight and the echoes of stolen memories.

Meridra lifted her hands, and as if in submission, the heavens replied. Dozens of ancient, floating scrolls burst to life around her, spiraling in graceful, synchronized orbits. With a delicate yet resolute flick of her fingers, the scrolls ignited in brilliant silver flames. These incandescent streaks of memory rained down upon the horde, and wherever the glyph-fire touched, the very essence of the Hollowkin convulsed and crumbled. Their bodies disintegrated into fluttering fragments, like pages of a well-worn tome torn apart by the relentless scribble of destiny.

Beside her, Christine's eyes shone with an otherworldly luminous white, their glow hinting at a being not entirely anchored in this realm. Her entire form pulsed with the rhythm of countless layered timelines; each version of herself danced on the edge of the present, steps half a heartbeat ahead or lingering just behind, flickering with every measured breath. She moved with the certainty and inevitability of prophecy unbound. With arms outstretched, she stepped forward and, with a fierce gesture, tore a ragged rift in the very fabric of the air.

From that jagged tear burst forth a maelstrom of elemental energy—sound, heat, and sheer will coalescing into a force that descended upon the battlefield like a fallen meteor. It struck the ground with explosive impact, sending the beleaguered Hollowkin sprawling in every direction. One creature—a bizarre amalgam of childlike form and spider-like appendages—leapt at her in a desperate bid for destruction. In a moment that seemed to stretch into eternity, Christine caught the creature mid-flight, murmured its true, whispered name, and watched, almost tenderly, as it unraveled into a fine dust, scattered to the winds of time.

"Fall back to the Memory Pillars!" Meridra bellowed, her voice resounding like thunder and the roar of an approaching storm. "Anchor the past before they can devour it entirely!"

At her command, Christine flung her arm outward, summoning a brilliant blast of golden light that arced gracefully like a divine blade. This radiant sweep cleaved through three charging Hollowkin with breathtaking precision. In the ensuing chaos, Simone, Theo, and Ingy tumbled to the ground beside her—breathless and battered, yet defiantly alive.

"You're still here?" Christine remarked with a triumphant grin, her voice rich with both exhaustion and fierce, unyielding fire.

"Where else would we be?" Simone panted, a wry smile breaking through the pain. "This is one hell of an apocalypse you're orchestrating."

Ingy staggered forward, his chest marked by glowing glyph scars that pulsed with urgency and secret histories. "They're trying to rip the glyph roots out of the earth. If they succeed… the field will collapse into oblivion."

"They won't get the chance," Meridra snarled, her tone a potent mixture of defiance and resolve.

In an instant, she conjured a column of pure, solid light and hurled it toward the distant horizon. When it struck, the impact was so profound that, for one perfect, suspended second, everything fell silent as if the world itself had paused—Hollowkin frozen mid-leap, the sky aglow with an intense, pulsing white light.

And then—

Boom.

The ground erupted in all directions, shattering into countless fragments. Memory rivers surged through the ruptured rock, cascading over the battlefield like a tidal wave composed entirely of raw, permeating narrative. The Hollowkin cried out—not in agony, but in a mournful recognition. One by one, they dissolved, not vanquished in death, but rewritten and transfigured; their stolen, corrupted forms sloughed away like ancient skin relinquishing its hold.

The momentum of battle shifted irrevocably.

Christine sank to one knee, her eyes flickering with the strain of untold battles. "I can't hold it much longer…"

"Then we end this now," Meridra declared without hesitation, summoning the very last vestiges of glyphlight into her grasp. With deliberate power, she molded it into a radiant sphere, as resplendent and vast as the heart of a distant moon.

"For Lizzie," Christine whispered, her tone heavy with the weight of both memory and the promise of tomorrow.

"For all of us," Meridra affirmed resolutely, and with one final, decisive throw, she launched the luminous orb straight into the very heart of the Merge Field.

Back in the Nexus, the Architect flinched violently. A sudden shockwave of betrayal and desperation surged through him, flickering like a dying star in the vast expanse of space, its light dimming with every pulse.

Lizzie's voice cut through the chaos with unwavering clarity, a beacon slicing through the cacophony of turmoil. "NOW, Asher!" she commanded, her tone sharp and resolute.

The two Ashers turned toward each other, their mirrored faces revealing stark contrasts. One appeared to tremble, his body a quivering mass of uncertainty, while the other seethed with barely contained rage, his eyes blazing with intensity. Despite their differences, both were alight with fear and poised for action. The air around them crackled with electric anticipation, charged with explosive energy that seemed to thrum in the very atmosphere.

"Merge with him and lose everything," Surface Asher whispered, his voice a fragile thread weaving through the turbulent storm that surrounded them.

"Merge with you," Acherra Asher countered, his words laced with determination, "and we find out who we really are."

With deliberate, fateful intent, they clasped hands, the motion heavy with finality and resolve.

And thus, the Merge began.

Glyphs erupted outward with unprecedented violence, a hurricane of furious symbols swirling through the Nexus like an avenging storm, their shapes twisting and turning with a ferocity unmatched. Blinding tendrils of light tore through the fractured scene, unraveling reality in a spectacular display of chaotic brilliance. The Ascension grid groaned under the pressure of the insurgent force, buckling as Lizzie flung her shard into the Anchor Core. There, time itself twisted and writhed, screaming in a silent, terrible symphony. The Unraveling Glyph exploded into being.

The Ascension grid collapsed in on itself.

The Architect's scream was a brutal cacophony, a symphony of anguish as his form splintered into a thousand fractured reflections. Each echo of himself rang out more desperate than the last, as his Crown shattered with a sound like the mournful weeping of distant stars.

And then—

Silence.

The Merge Field trembled, absorbing the chaos in an aftershock of cataclysmic consequence, before finally stilling.

Asher emerged—whole, radiant, real—standing beside Lizzie. His breath rose like smoke in the cooling air, his appearance familiar yet subtly altered, with hair now an inky black and eyes gleaming a piercing blue. Theo and

Simone stumbled into view, coughing amidst the settling dust, while Ingy limped behind them, a testament to the trials they had endured.

"Did it work?" Theo asked before suddenly pulling up short at the sight of Asher. "Dude, what happened to you?"

Lizzie met Asher's eyes.

"We're still here," she whispered.

Asher smiled. "Let's finish this."

Chapter 19: Collapse

The Merge Field crumpled inward with a resounding, earth-shattering pulse, as if the very fabric of existence had been squeezed and torn at the same time. What had once promised the taste of victory instead erupted into utter devastation. The Ascension ritual—the desperate, impossible act of balance mixed with defiance—had not brought harmony but fractured reality into a thousand jagged fragments. Glyphs whirled away from their orbits like splintered constellations, brutally reshaping space into razor-like edges. The proud, revered Hollow Crown had shattered, and the Architect had fallen from grace. Yet, in a twist defying expectation, he did not simply perish.

Instead, he transformed. From the collapsing ruins of the Ascension grid emerged his new form—a cyclone of intricate fractal geometry fused with swirling liquid obsidian. He became a living wound in the tapestry of reality, a vortex that drew in shards of splintered timelines and anguished matter. His cry was no longer a mere sound; it had evolved into a cataclysmic breach in dimensions—a rupture capable of shattering both thought and distance.

Around the Nexus, the Hollowkin convulsed in fitful spasms. Their forms splintered apart as if made of delicate glass, their skin warping and cracking, held together only by the echoing remnants of forgotten memories. Some of them howled as their bodies unraveled under the weight of disintegration, while others grotesquely swelled as they absorbed fragments of collapsing, dying worlds.

The ritual had not ended the Merge—it had merely undone the lock that had held it in place. With that, the Architect was unbound, free to reshape reality as he saw fit.

A violent shriek, born from the unstable, writhing air, tore across the Merge Field as the storm raged on, a voracious maelstrom that consumed both stars and the sky alike. Lizzie, alongside the two Ashers, struggled to hold their ground against the relentless onslaught, their eyes straining to shield themselves from debris that had materialized from nothing—chunks of buildings, disembodied faces of people, entire lives dislodged from the steady pulse of reality like puzzle pieces flung apart in chaos.

Then, amidst the carnage, came the light. A portal, rimmed with glyphs and spiraling open near the fractured edge of the storm, erupted into being. From it stepped Meridra, her cloak tattered and worn, with ancient scrolls trailing behind her like the luminous tails of comets. Following her was Christine, her eyes aglow with layered starlight and a burning halo of memory-energy that danced around her back, as if marking her with divine purpose.

They looked every bit the warriors who had just waded through an apocalypse—and bore the hardened readiness to do it all again.

"The ritual didn't work," Meridra declared without a hint of preamble. Her voice rang out sharp and flat, reminiscent of a bell that had cracked at its core, its sound lingering like a ghost.

"We know," Asher responded grimly. "He's absorbing the instability. He's becoming... something worse."

Christine's eyes narrowed as she fixed her gaze on the ever-growing mass of the Architect, whose twisted form spiraled higher with every stolen second. "He's no longer tethered by the glyph anchors. That crown was never meant to imprison him—it was a spark, a fuse waiting to ignite."

Stepping forward, Lizzie's hands trembled yet remained resolute. "Then what do we do? The Merge Field is collapsing around us. If we don't stop this—"

Before she could finish, Christine pulled her into a fierce, protective embrace. "You and Asher must heal the rift. But it won't be enough—not now."

Meridra's expression was grave as she nodded, her voice heavy with the weight of destiny. "The Ascension has splintered across realms. Now, our only hope is to complete the ritual on two fronts: here, within the depths of the Merge Field, and above, where the Hollowkin have breached the surface tether."

Christine turned toward the swirling chaos at the field's edge, where multiple Hollowkin shimmered into view, transitioning in and out of Acherra and Southridge like erratic static on an old screen. "We'll take to the surface.

Theo, Simone, Ingy, and I will drive the Hollowkin into a binding zone at the school. Once we're inside, we can activate a counter-ritual—one that will anchor their essence within a glyph prism, forcing them back beneath the earth."

Meridra interjected, her tone as firm as it was resolute, "But that will only succeed if you stabilize the central rift and sever the Architect's core anchor from below."

Lizzie's gaze shifted between her comrades, her throat tightening as the enormity of their task settled upon her. "So we're dividing our efforts again. But this time... we simply cannot fail."

With that, Christine drew Lizzie close into a sudden, fierce embrace. "We won't fail. I trust you, Lizzie. I always have. Now trust me too."

Meridra's gaze moved steadily to Asher as she offered him one final look, measured and deliberate. "You are more than a Merge, Asher. You are a bridge between worlds. Let that truth guide you now."

Asher's eyes widened with sudden understanding. "If all of us are taking up this mantle, then what will you do?"

With a gentle tenderness mingled with resolute strength, Meridra looked upon her son, her smile a bittersweet blend of pride and sorrow as she brushed his face with her hand. "Someone must stand against the Architect; if I don't, none of you will have a chance."

"But I just got you back! I'm whole now. We can finally be a family again," he pleaded, tears glistening down his cheeks as they tracked along his face.

Drawing him into a warm, consoling embrace, she pressed a soft kiss to his forehead and smiled with quiet joy as she cradled his hopes. "We always have been a family."

And with that, they were gone—stepping back through the swirling portal, enveloped in a burst of radiant light as they vanished toward the shattered remnants of the town above.

Lizzie's eyes locked onto Asher's before shifting to the storm that loomed ahead. "You heard her," she stated firmly, her voice hardening with unyielding resolve. "Let's finish what we started."

A Storm of Worlds

Lizzie and the newly Merged Asher stood at the trembling edge of the Merge Field, looking toward the storm at the heart of Acherra.

It wasn't just a storm—it was all storms. A spinning singularity of failed timelines, screaming souls, and seething glyphlight. Trees from Southridge blinked in and out of glowing white soil. A classroom door spiraled through the air like a tossed coin.

Somewhere, a school bus blinked—half metal, half bone. Lizzie's breath came in ragged gasps, the enormity of what they faced looming larger with each passing second. It was too much. She could feel it—freedom was within reach, yet slipping further away, even as they stared at it head on.

Asher, heart pounding, spoke into the churning void. "We're not enough." His new voice carried more than just sound; it was a perfect blend of memory and magic, of time lost and refound.

Lizzie heard the truth in his words and felt it echo deep within her bones. "I can feel it—he's growing faster than we can stop."

Then came the voice—her voice. The same as Lizzie's, but older. More broken. More whole.

"I know."

Lizzie's doppelgänger stepped through the chaos like a mirror slicing through smoke. She was exactly Lizzie, and yet not—her glyphs were brighter, her eyes wiser, her soul tempered in flame. She cut through the bedlam with elegantly deliberate strides, a haunting vision from a future that had once felt inevitable and was now unbearably real. Lizzie stared, her own soul screaming in recognition. The rush of past and future collided within her, spinning like a violent cyclone.

This was her—and something more. A possibility. A path she had not yet taken but could already feel seeping through every fiber of her being.

"I've seen the end," the other Lizzie said quietly. "We all did. You can't fix it without all of you."

She extended a hand.

Lizzie froze, her heart racing. Could this really be? A reflection from another, darker timeline? A lifeline from parts of herself she had thought forever lost? Her fingers trembled as she reached out and took what was being offered.

A spark of understanding flashed.

"You've been with me this whole time..." Lizzie said suddenly, her mind racing, putting the pieces together.

"There it is," her doppel said with a crooked smile, watching Lizzie work it out and smile back.

She had been two this whole time. Two souls overlapping, interwoven, each straining for their own future but knowing they could truly be one.

They share a kindred smile...and merged.

There was no pain. Only clarity. Two streams converging into a flood. Two girls, two destinies, now woven into one unified thread. A whirlwind of perception rushed through her, a kaleidoscope of all storms, all worlds, all selves converging into one undeniable truth. Lizzie saw it all, and at last, she understood.

Lizzie blinked—and the world shifted.

On the Surface: War and Glyphfire

In Southridge, the gates of hell had swung wide open. Flames danced with furious intensity, casting horrifying shadows over collapsing realms as Simone, Theo, Ingy, Christine, and Meridra sprinted desperately through the inferno. They barreled forward like human war machines, adeptly steering waves of twisting, mutating Hollowkin toward the sanctuary of the school.

"They're regrouping!" Simone bellowed, her voice raw with determination as she wielded her glowing glyph-dagger like a radiant scythe against the onslaught. With each sweeping arc, her blade cleaved through the contorted, warping spines of the Hollowkin, sending shards of their grotesque forms scattering into the ash-choked air. "Push them to the field!"

Theo skidded to her side in a burst of urgency, his glyph-scroll blazing with the intensity of a handheld sun. Its brilliant light illuminated the darkness as he explained, "The glyphs must be activated in precise sequence—parking lot, auditorium, roof, gym, and then the center field! If we miss even one step, Asher can't perform the final embed!" His words were punctuated by the roar of clashing powers and the frantic beat of their hearts.

Meanwhile, Ingy was a whirlwind of determination, his form a spectral blur as he phased in and out of sight. He struck with lethal precision, infiltrating the very essence of the Hollowkin and dismantling them from within. In a stunning display of raw power, he tore a tentacled aberration from the fiery sky and hurled it into a nearby SUV like a searing meteor, the impact echoing like thunder through the chaos.

"I'll hold the courtyard," Ingy snarled, his voice dripping with defiance despite blood trickling from his mouth.

"They're attempting to breach the nexus root!" His tone was as ferocious as the battle raging all around him.

High above the gymnasium roof, Christine floated gracefully, defying gravity as shards of fragmented memories spiraled around her like serrated blades. With a voice laced with urgency, she warned all, "He's coming! They want to rewrite us—every one of us! Not today!" Her words hung in the air, imbued with the fierce promise of resistance.

Meridra, ever the embodiment of ancient power, exchanged a resolute nod with Christine before soaring into the turbulent sky. In that moment, the Architect materialized—a haunting presence surveying the battlefield as the group darted erratically from one crumbling building to another in search of the indispensable glyphs while fending off the relentless Hollowkin.

The ensuing clash between Meridra and the Architect was epic—a titanic ballet of might and sorcery. Meridra radiated with the glow of primeval energy, her ancient scrolls orbiting around her like furious comets. With a defiant cry, she slammed her palms into the earth, sending a searing ripple across the cracked asphalt that triggered brilliant explosions of light and shards of glass as the Hollowkin were obliterated in cascading showers.

Not to be outdone, the Architect unleashed harsh beams of purple energy. One such devastating ray struck Meridra, hurling her across the sprawling football field. Theo, Simone, and Ingy cried out in horrified unison as the

Architect's laughter—cold, mocking, and filled with cruel delight—reverberated through the smoky battlefield.

"THEO!" Christine shouted, her voice cutting through the tumult. "Glyph two is lit. GO! There's nothing else you can do here. We've got this—so you and Simone must reach the final glyph!" Her determination was palpable, a beacon of hope amidst chaos.

The Architect sneered at her with disdain. "You've got nothing, young one," he jeered, his tone dripping with contempt. But Christine, quick and cunning, launched herself into the air with the sudden force of a tempest. In one fluid motion, she delivered a spinning, dynamic kick to his jaw, simultaneously summoning a gnarled tree from the earth. With a burst of telepathic might, she forced the enormous oak—its roots entwined with elemental power—to slam into the Architect's chest, sending him crashing violently through the nearby scoreboard.

This burst of defiance provided a brief but precious reprieve. Then, without warning, the air around Christine began to sizzle. Electricity crackled fiercely in a violent explosion of energy that hurled her through the air, a helpless body crashing into a parked bus with a resounding impact.

Hovering ominously above, the Architect fixed his menacing gaze, his eyes alight with unbridled hate. It was in this grim moment that he observed Lizzie and Asher were conspicuously absent. A look of enraged betrayal twisted his features as he roared in seething anger before evaporating in a flash of swirling purple smoke, leaving a vacuous void in his wake.

The Merge Glyph

Inside the storm, Lizzie and Asher pushed toward the collapsing Anchor Nexus with an urgency that defied time and space. Every desperate breath they took cost them precious seconds; every fleeting second cost them yet another collapsing layer of Southridge. Its existence flickered more faintly as they inched closer to their goal. The world was a snow globe in the hands of a cruel child, shaking violently with each heartbeat.

Every Hollowkin that was unfortunate enough to lash out at them was struck down without thought, like gnats in a storm.

"I see it," Lizzie said with electric intensity—her eyes blazing white with glyphlight, her veins breathing new life as runes coursed through them. "The Architect's feeding on the world's roots. If we can't cut him off..."

"Then everything Merges," Asher concluded with grim certainty, his voice a mix of urgency and newfound authority. Every word was a scalpel, cutting closer to the heart of their impossible task.

The Architect loomed before them, a spiral of rage and immeasurable power. This was not just an adversary; it was a towering figure made of all selves, every version that should never have existed, now twisting hatefully into one singular horror. It embodied the nightmares of all the worlds it wished to destroy.

"I AM THE ANSWER," it roared, its voice like ten thousand storms. "I AM THE MERGE."

Then—with malevolent speed—it lunged, a torrent of raw will and destructive intention.

Lizzie raised the glyph shard in a defiant arc. Asher extended his arms, his hands glowing with the essence of time and memory. Together, they called the Anchor Glyph. It responded to their call with a brilliance that transcended sight—from the sky, it came—a beam of spiraling logic, pure intent, and fractal memory. Time itself seemed to hesitate, waiting to witness the outcome.

From the school field, Theo and Simone were fighting to get to the glyph point. Four crazed Hollowkin rose up before them, eyes filled with menace and rage.

"We're not gonna make it!" Theo bellowed, his voice shaking with desperation as he lashed out at Simone. Her eyes mirrored helpless determination as she fought to keep the encroaching threat at bay, but even her valiant efforts were beginning to wane. They had been tantalizingly close to their goal.

Glyph three—the final glyph—shimmered across the barren, scorched expanse of the parking lot, its eerie glow piercing through the ascendant chaos like a steadfast lighthouse amid a raging, disordered sea. Yet now, four imposing Hollowkin obstructed their path, rising from the fissured, ruptured asphalt as if conjured from a fever dream. They emerged like nightmares wrought in spilled ink and shattered glass, their eyes burning not merely red but seething with a primal, interdimensional fury.

In a frenzied bid for salvation, Theo raised his glyph scroll, its intended spark of hope sputtering ineffectually. At the same moment, Simone's dagger flickered with the last vestiges of its charge, a beacon on the verge of extinguishing. Suddenly, one of the Hollowkin shrieked—a sound of pure, unholy terror—and charged forward, its limb-tendrils unfurling in a spiraling blaze of black flame.

Theo braced himself, his heart hammering. "If we die, I'm blaming you—!" he shouted, the words cut short by a resounding BOOM.

A flash of blinding white light exploded in the midst of the chaos, its brilliance so intense that it kissed the darkness with ephemeral hope, vaporizing one of the monstrous beings in a ghastly, silenced shriek. As the smoke and sparks parted, a lone figure emerged, striding through the billowing haze with the gravitas of legend—as if torn from the annals of a war-torn tapestry. It was Kai Tran.

This was not the Kai who had vanished into the ether weeks ago; he now appeared transformed. Donning weathered Acherra battle gear embroidered with intricate glyph-bands and etched with luminous crystal streaks, his presence was otherworldly. His chestplate glimmered with swirling, looping runes, and a gauntlet on his left arm pulsed with an almost sentient power. His once bewildered gaze had sharpened into eyes burning with resolute purpose as he gripped a formidable two-handed, glyph-forged glaive as though it were a part of him.

"Hope you weren't about to surrender," Kai called out, his voice imbued with calm authority and unruffled coolness.

Simone's mouth fell open in astonishment. "Kai?!" she gasped.

In a seamless, balletic motion, Kai twirled his glaive and lunged forward with blinding speed. Two of the Hollowkin fell in rapid succession—a sizzling arc of searing energy cleaving one in half, while another was impaled and shattered until it dissolved into an oily, sinister mist. The final creature reeled back with a guttural snarl, only to be struck with a resounding impact as a glowing crystal disc, launched from Kai's charged gauntlet, slammed into its head with the resonant chime of a bell tolling backward.

"Whoa!" Theo shouted in incredulous awe. "Dude, you're alive?!"

Kai turned with a crooked, knowing grin that spoke of battles survived and mysteries unraveled. "Last I checked. I'm just a little... edgier now."

Simone, still reeling from the raw magnetism of his return, stammered, "What happened to you? You were—gone. And now you're... what, some kind of magical super soldier?!"

With a nonchalant swipe, Kai wiped streaks of ichor off his blade. "Long story. I got sucked into a nightmare dimension where everything was made of sentient oil—

utterly repulsive. Then, out of the viscous chaos, a fearsome boss lady appeared. Her face was like a thundercloud chiseled from marble, and she barked, 'stop sulking and start slicing,' or I'd be marooned in that goo realm forever. So, I picked up a glaive."

Theo shook his head in both disbelief and admiration. "That is as horrifying as it is absurdly awesome."

"Story of my life," Kai replied with a dismissive flick of his wrist, scattering a shard of Hollowkin off his pauldron. "So, what's the plan?"

Still gathering her wits after the overwhelming surge of Kai-ness, Simone pointed toward the pulsating, radiant glyph point glimmering fifty feet away. "Activate the third glyph. Or everything collapses."

"Easy," Kai affirmed, launching into a sprint that blurred his form as he bore down the distance with relentless urgency.

Theo turned to Simone, wide-eyed with incredulity. "You really think I can get banished to the goo world and come back looking half as cool?"

Simone replied deadpanned, "You'd probably trip on entry."

"Valid," Theo conceded with a rueful smile.

Moments later, the glyph point erupted in an explosion of incandescent light, bathing the area in a celestial glow. Kai stood alongside it, casually dusting his hands as though he had just completed the most mundane of tasks.

"Let's do this," he declared, his voice steady and resolute.

And together, with hearts pounding and destinies entwined, they raced forward toward the final convergence and with a wild leap Theo jammed the final glyph-scroll into the anchor point with frantic determination, his hands moving like lightning.

The glyph network across the town blazed into life, a conflagration of light and sound.

Back in the Mergestorm, Asher took a breath, steeled his resolve.

And embedded the new glyph. The sigil was fighting against him, part of it wanting to merge and the other half refusing to be made whole.

Then Asher felt a hand on his. Lizzie smiled up at him, "thought you could use a hand."

Asher smiled back, the glyph was no longer resistant, it hungered for completion.

Time exploded.

And Then—

—silence, splitting the world like lightning.

Every forced Merge—the ones trapped, twisted, incomplete—severed. All fractured timelines splintered apart. Every wrongly bound soul blazed with recognition as they were released back to the worlds they had been torn from.

The Hollowkin cracked like mirrors, shattering in bloom-like shapes, and vanished into memory. A soft wind carried their ghostly dust into air that was suddenly free of smoke. The storm began to slow.

Lizzie fell to her knees. Her breath came ragged, each inhalation a small triumph. Asher stood beside her, radiant, complete, glowing with possibility. He was the sum of all versions, the answer to all paths.

"You did it," Lizzie whispered, barely finding the breath.

"No," Asher said, looking toward the field, the sky, the friends who held the line. "We did."

They exchanged a look of shared victory, the briefest moment of relief.

And then the world burst. Like ten thousand roaring cannons. Like annihilation.

The Architect roared in fury, then in disbelief, and finally in fear as his fractured body was pulled into the closing rift.

An enormous explosion engulfed Acherra. All-consuming walls of light and sound rushed toward them, a tidal wave of devastation roaring toward their fragile moment of hope. Lizzie and Asher braced for the impact.

Chapter 20: What Remains

The storm passed. The kind that rattled not just windows but realities. The kind that downed not just power lines but worlds. The kind that reshaped lives and memories, and bent existence itself—leaving splinters, cracks, and unexpected connections in its wake.

In Southridge, the residents awoke the next morning with only vague recollections of the chaos that had left them reeling. Downed branches littered the streets, flickering lights haunted the houses with ghostly persistence, and dreams stretched like shadows long into waking. They were nightmares they couldn't quite remember but couldn't shake, unsettling visions that clung to their consciousness like cobwebs that refused to be brushed away.

On the local news, Mayor Everard stood with great self-importance beside a crumbling sinkhole that had conveniently sealed itself overnight. He called it an "unusual but natural geologic correction," concocting a grand narrative about gas pockets and tectonic shifts. "We've had worse in the seventies," he chuckled, patting a bemused rescue worker's helmet like he'd personally saved the day.

But beneath his easy explanations, others whispered. They remembered things too strange to dismiss—blinding flashes of impossible light, streetlamps bending eerily toward the sky, and shadowy figures with too many arms walking backward through their living rooms. A few swore they heard singing beneath the earth, voices layered in forgotten languages that resonated with an ancient familiarity.

And every one of them, without exception, dreamed wildly, vividly, obsessively of mirrors.

The Ascension had been stopped, the cosmic upheLizziel frozen in an impossible standoff.

The universes did not collapse into one another, shredding fabric and form, nor did they peel away into nothingness. They persisted instead in a new, uncharted coexistence, as though gigantic trees with interlocked roots, each firmly its own but sharing earth, water, and life beneath the surface.

Despite the cataclysm, Acherra did not devour the surface world, nor did it lose itself to oblivion. The realms remained, keenly aware of their own separateness. But now there were crossings.

Living ones.

Within the sprawling, disoriented landscape of the newly joined worlds, Christine Marlowe found herself suspended in uncertainty and echoes. After her plunge through the bus, she had woken to discover existence had rewritten itself, the two realms running now side-by-side like parallel tracks.

At times, she felt as if she were moving through layers of herself, each fraction of her soul whispering against the others, the resonance of her own being nearly overwhelming. There were moments she would glance at her reflection and not recognize her own face. The angle of her smile, the hue of her thoughts—it was as if they belonged to another, like strange versions of herself bleeding over from alternate lives.

Sometimes, when she was least prepared, Christine answered questions before they were asked, Lizzie's words crystallizing in her mind before sound touched air. At others, she felt Meridra's wisdom seep into her dreams. In this fragile new order, where identities brushed against their counterparts, she could feel the tether between the worlds, as real and vital as blood pulsing in her veins.

She knew that something profound had shifted. She knew they would never be the same. Beneath the dense weave of possibility, the realms began to heal. Acherra was its own again, but different. Its time was no longer stolen. Unraveled timelines twined together, became whole.

Before the explosion, Ingy had been ready to give himself, ready to spend every shred of existence to halt the Merge. He fought with that reckless abandon, expecting this to be the final fight. Instead, he had awoken—bruised and worthy—under the violet sky. Like Christine, Ingy was changed, but still himself.

Ingy remained behind in the borderland between the realms, taking up quiet watch at the edge of the Glyphwake. He had earned peace, but still bore Hollowkin eyes. A remnant. A bridge. A guardian of those who might yet stumble through the seams.

Acherra, the brilliant realm of endless possibility, began to regrow. It was wounded, yes, but defiantly alive. Across the land, the effects of the dreadful near-Ascension were visible and raw, yet there was an air of determined resilience. The majestic crystal forests, once gleaming and proud, lay scorched and ruined by the relentless push of the Merge. The shimmering glyph rivers, the veins of the world, had dried to whispers. Their once vigorous flows now reduced to mere trickles, faint and gasping. Even so, the spirit of renewal was undeniable. Already, delicate sprouts of bioluminescent moss began to curl their fragile tendrils up the shattered marble pillars near the ruins of the Merge Field. The memory-trees, gnarled and wise, showed signs of life as they dared to bloom again. They did so with the caution of a realm that had nearly seen its own end. Carefully. Hesitantly.

Meridra walked alone among them, her steps light but meaningful. She had refused to return to the surface world, choosing instead to become the Keeper of What Had Almost Been. Her scrolls, repositories of ancient power and wisdom, sang differently now. No longer loud with the urgency to prevent calamity, their songs resonated low and mournful, their tones patient and enduring. She was determined to remain. To exist in a space between remembering and forgetting. She would wait, bravely and quietly, in case her presence was needed again.

Kai Tran lingered at the edge of his driveway, caught between disbelief and longing as he looked at the house he hadn't seen in what felt like a lifetime. It appeared...

ordinary. The porch light flickered above the welcome mat with an almost indifferent rhythm. A faded basketball lay abandoned in the overgrown yard, and the same cracked garden gnome by the mailbox seemed to sneer, its crooked gaze accusing him of forgetfulness. There were no lingering oily shadows, no remnants of warped reflections, no glassy-eyed figures waiting in grotesque mimicry.

Yet, as he stepped inside, unease knotted in his gut. "Kai!" his mother's call drifted from the kitchen, as light and caring as ever, as if time itself had been oblivious to the changes. "You missed dinner—again. I saved you some lasagna."

His father appeared from around the corner, a friendly smile and a spoon in hand. "Storm kept you out late? Crazy night, huh?"

Kai paused, his heart heavy with the burden of unspoken truths. They looked the same, sounded the same. But they weren't Machina—not anymore. Their expressions, free from the eerie perfection that once defined them, now flickered with genuine emotion and uncertain hesitation. And yet, everything felt off, as if a part of him was trapped in a discordant melody.

"Yeah," Kai replied with a slow, conflicted tone as he removed his boots, each movement weighted with hesitation. "Crazy storms."

His mother frowned ever so slightly, scrutinizing him. "You look tired, sweetheart. Rough night?"

He nodded, swallowing hard. "Weird dreams."

Her laughter, light and dismissive, cut through the murk of his memories. "Us too. I dreamt your father was made of wires and asked me for toast three hundred times."

His dad chuckled, joining the fragile mirth. "I dreamed I was stuck in a vending machine. Couldn't get anyone to pick me."

They laughed, a sound too bright and untouched. Kai forced a smile that never reached his eyes, troubled by the duality of his reality. As he ascended the stairs in silence, their laughter trailed behind him like echoes from a life he could no longer recognize—a life marked by false comfort and uneasy truths.

His room was just as he'd left it: posters peeling at the corners, clothes scattered, an abandoned half-finished comic on the desk. But in the far corner—propped against the wall with a silent insistence that defied explanation—rested the glaive. Its blade emitted a faint, almost reluctant gleam in the gloom, while glyphs crawled across its surface like hesitant dreams come to life.

Kai sat on his bed, his gaze fixed on the weapon. In that moment, the conflict within him deepened. He hadn't told Theo or Simone everything. Not the dark, hidden part that whispered in his dreams—dreams swollen with oily textures, incessant humming, and a palpable life of their own. The part where, in a disconcerting moment of intimacy and fear, a strange woman with hollow eyes and a voice that thundered in silk had leaned in close. Her hand on his chest, her words embedded in his every breath: "I will require more from you in the future, Kai Tran."

There had been neither a smile nor a threat in her tone, only an unsettling promise that resonated with painful certainty. He rubbed the back of his neck, the motion both a comfort and a seizure, and looked away, torn between the desire to forget and the not-quite-vanished pull of that memory.

Outside, the wind stirred the trees as thunder rumbled in the distance—lazy yet laden with an ominous promise. Kai stole a glance back at the glaive, his voice barely a whisper, "I'm not so sure I ever want to find out."

Yet, deep within the cold metal, something pulsed—a quiet, conflicting heartbeat that mocked his indecision. And as much as he wished it were different, Kai couldn't shake the feeling that it no longer cared what he wanted. Not anymore.

And then there was Lizzie.

Merged now. Whole. Alive in a way that startled her. Like a voice that knows a single line of the song, she felt more certain. More complete. This was how it was supposed to be. She stood at the crest of the drive-in hill on a gray morning, the sun rising like a whisper through the trees. The slanted hole behind her no longer glowed—but she could still feel the pulse beneath it, like a heartbeat inside the earth. Her glyph shard was gone. She no longer needed it. The runes had taken up residence along her arms and spine, faint and living things that pulsed gently when she dreamed. She wore them like bruises from a beautiful struggle, souvenirs of the battles that had nearly broken them all.

Everything had changed—and nothing had. School was still in session. The gas station reopened.

Simone talked a little too loudly in class and passed Lizzie notes that said things like, "Still not over my ghost twin. Also, I want boba."

Theo pretended he hadn't cried during the final glyph ritual, but now read ancient glyph scrolls in secret and was trying to teach the chess club how to hex their opponents "just a little."

Lizzie found herself laughing at the jokes, at the notes, at the hexes. She looked at her friends, her classes, her life, and was filled with currents of the unstolen. Of the real. Yet her thoughts were drawn again and again to the lives she might have lived, the lives they might have had, the paths that flickered just beyond sight.

She remembered the moment before the Merge failed, before Asher answered the riddle of his own existence. She remembered the look in his eyes when he was finally whole. She baked him cookies, a bad attempt and a worse apology. The crumbs leaving a trail back to the drive-in.

Asher chose to stay.

He stood now outside his home on Quarry Lane, where the porch light cast a familiar glow, flickering dutifully in Morse-code comfort as his robotic parents greeted him with their usual glitchy warmth. They had been resynced, slightly. Their firmware updated.

Even so, a small hiss of static accompanied each welcome. A new echo of life yet remembered.

Mr. Quinn now told jokes. Bad ones. Most were old, recycled, and brought back to life, like the rest of them. "Been the usual Merge of a day? Another round of devastation for dinner?" He seemed quite pleased with himself, even though both parents spoke at once, and their voices still overlapped.

"We've updated the calendar and marked it with your survivals," they said together, pixelated and doting.

They'd taken to calling both versions of Asher "Son Prime," which made absolutely no sense and still managed to cover all possibilities—which made absolutely no sense and somehow still worked.

Lizzie had called from across the neighborhood through their connection, her voice clear as if she were beside him, yet another power she was going to have to get used to. "So which is it? Are you both? Neither?"

Asher hesitated, then laughed. "I think I'm both," Asher had finally told her, a few days after it all ended. "And neither. And honestly, I'm okay with that."

He smiled then, a new Asher-smile that felt older, wiser, and finally unburdened. It was the sort of smile only the unstolen can make. Only those without fracture. "I just want to be here," he added, the words like promises. "For a while. You know. Try normal."

There was a pause on the other end, a pause that seemed to stretch through memories. Lizzie had nodded like he could see. "Let me know how that goes," she said, her voice half a laugh, half a wish.

He could almost hear the relief trail behind her words like a comet's tail.

At night, she wrote. Not in a journal, and not in a scroll—but in glyphs. Secret ones. Memory-bound ones. They curled across her ceiling in lines that glowed only when the moon hit them just right. She inscribed names: Asher. Meridra. Simone. Theo. Her mom. Ingy.

Even the Architect—though she left his glyph cracked. She wrote with elegant, looping certainty. She wrote with the kind of confidence that only the stitched-together have.

At the very center, Lizzie carved a single, spiraling word in looping silver light: REMEMBER.

Her mother had suffered during the fight with the Architect and Lizzie knew that full recovery was a long way off, but she also knew that she would be by her mom's side the entire way.

Beneath the floorboards of the town, in a place no one could name, something stirred—but did not wake. Not yet. A remnant. A slumbering seam. Because for now... peace was enough. And Lizzie would make sure it stayed that way.

Epilogue: Reflected

It began with a mirror. Not the ordinary kind that hangs above a bathroom sink or in the fitting rooms at the bustling mall. This one was ancient—imbued with an air of wisdom, perhaps—and buried deep beneath layers of fractured time, far beneath the forgotten town of Southridge where the earth had long ago lost its memory of its own name.

In the depths, there were no footsteps to be heard. No wind stirred the stillness. Just a flicker. A delicate shimmer danced in the air, reminiscent of heat rising off asphalt, though the ground here hadn't basked in sunlight for millennia. The mirror—cracked but not shattered—stood resolutely in the hollow of a cavern, its walls adorned with forgotten glyphs and interwoven with bleeding roots. Its surface pulsed faintly, not with light, but with the weight of memory. It remembered. And it was remembering Lizzie.

Her name unfurled like tendrils of smoke across the glass, curling into shapes that were both familiar and strange.

Elsewhere, in the thin boundary between the shadowy realm of Acherra and the surface world, something shifted. It wasn't the Hollowkin—no, they had mostly vanished now, their resonance dissipated, their voracious hunger silenced. This was something different. Something colder. Quieter. It didn't crawl; it seeped like a chilling fog.

A whisper slipped through a newly formed room, one that hadn't existed mere seconds before. "Too early," intoned a voice that echoed like the sound of splintered bells chiming in dissonance. "She is not ready."

Another voice, slick and supple like oil gliding over velvet, responded, "But she is remembering. And they are remembering her."

Silence descended.

And then, a third voice—a presence that did not communicate with words but with pure sensation—spoke. It conveyed meaning through the feeling of standing precariously at the edge of a cliff, in the insistent pull of gravity, in the forgotten rhythm of a second heartbeat.

The cycle is not complete.

In Southridge, Lizzie stirred restlessly in her sleep, her eyes darting beneath closed lids in a frantic dance. In the dream, she found herself standing in a field composed of mirrorgrass—each blade sharp enough to slice thought away from memory. Above her, six versions of herself floated like ethereal constellations, each wearing a distinct expression. The sixth one wept with silent tears. The fifth one laughed with abandon. The second whispered urgently, "Run."

And looming above them all, a seventh reflection stood inverted, its body faceless, its arms stretched unnaturally long. It watched with an intensity that pierced through the dreamscape.

She awoke with a jolt, a gasp escaping her lips, her heart pounding like a warning bell tolling in the night.

The glyphs on her ceiling glowed with a faint luminescence in response. One of them—just one—was new. She hadn't carved it. She didn't recognize it.

It resembled an eye, and it was wide open, watching.

About the Author

I had dreamed of being a writer ever since I was a little boy growing up in Northeast Texas. My imagination has always been wild and carefree. My first typewriter was a little plastic blue toy typewriter when I was 10 years old. I wore that thing out writing stories and screenplays, even though I didn't know the first thing how to do so. When I was in high school, I told myself and my friends that I would write a novel one day, and then life happened. All these years later most of those friends are gone, and here I am, still writing in their memory, still creating stories from dreams, jokes, and conversations. From time to time I revisit that little boy who used to gaze out into the night, when the fireflies were blinking their summer dance, and imagine what was out there.

Now I live in North Mississippi and one thing remains true: There are many more stories to tell.

www.ingramcontent.com/pod-product-compliance
Lightning Source LLC
Chambersburg PA
CBHW051950220626
47052CB00004B/874